# Broken Promises.
## By Sarah Barnard

First edition 2013

ISBN-13: 978-1494277208

ISBN-10: 1494277204

Published by Osier Publishing

www.osierpublishing.co.uk

First published 2013

© Copyright Sarah Barnard 2006

The moral rights of the author and artist have been asserted.

All rights reserved.

No part of this publication may be reproduced, stored in a retrieval system, or transmitted in any form or by any means, electronic, mechanical or otherwise, without the written permission of the publisher or author.

All characters and locations within this work are fictitious and any resemblance to real people or places is entirely coincidental.

Cover design by J Hunter at Osier Publishing.

Pile of paper image from the cover by anankkml at freedigitalphotos.net

# Thanks

Gratitude is due to the usual suspects, and a few extras too.

Broken Promises began life in 2006 and is being released 7 years later. It's been a hard book to finish and get ready, for so many reasons. Kris, as always in the Portal series, it's all your fault! Claire, who I've now lost touch with, who badgered me with questions about what happened to cause the rage and pain in The Portal Between. I don't know where you are now, but thank you.

Mel and Krystie who helped polish the text, find errors and provide feedback. Anything we've missed between us is now down to me. You did a great job, thank you.

Family and friends who continue to put up with my distraction, flights of fancy, and disappearance for hours on end into a world of my own imagination. Thank you.

Broken Promises is dedicated to anyone who has escaped, is escaping, or is still within, an abusive relationship. I seem to have known more than my fair share of people in that situation, or maybe there are more than we realise.

I wish you all the help and strength you need to rebuild the life you deserve. Even on the darkest days, stay strong, there is light to be found in time.

# Contents

1. Leaving
2. Living
3. Rules
4. Control
5. Rebellion
6. Locked up
7. Do what you have to
8. Discovered
9. Name
10. Escape

# 1. Leaving

It was the first day back at school for all the children after the long summer holidays and Kate had a couple of hours to herself, but she simply sat at the kitchen table with a large mug of tea. Cradling the warmth in her hands, she let the heat spread calmly through her.

Kate startled at a knock on the kitchen door. She wasn't expecting anyone. Wearily dragging herself from the chair, she slowly pulled open the door.

"Lily, come in." Kate's voice was tired and flat. Lily frowned in concern. Perhaps this wasn't the best time.

*The events of the past few years had changed Kate. Lily could see rawness and fragility in her friend which hadn't been there before. There was grey in her hair and lines on her face etched there by pain and grief. They matched Lily's own smattering of grey which wove through dark hair that still held copper glints in the right light.*

*Lily looked down at the roll of loose pages in her hands. She hadn't read all of it, but she'd skimmed some of it after Elder had given the document to her as she left that place for the last time. The last Portal she'd opened, bringing Kate and Susan home after Gentian's daughter had been born.*

*Then her own magic had died.*

*"Hi, Kate." Lily spoke softly and the tone in her voice made Kate suddenly become more alert.*

*"What's wrong?" she asked, a frown creasing her face and worry standing in her eyes. "Lily?" Kate searched her friend's face for an answer. Lily came to the table and sat. She placed the document on the table and left it there in between them.*

*"It's from Sam," Lily said, watching Kate's face fight to not crumple into tears. "She wrote it for you before she died. It's an account of what happened while Ametsam held her." Kate stared at the roll of pages. Lily reached over to pat Kate's shoulder gently. "I'll put the kettle on," she said and got up to walk across the kitchen. Lily leaned on the worktop and listened to the kettle heat up. She watched as Kate pushed out a trembling hand to touch the paper. The tightly rolled pages slowly began to uncurl to reveal familiar handwriting which crawled across each page.*

My name was Sam Brewer and I was thirty-one when I discovered I had never been who I thought I was. Now I have no idea who I am supposed to be.

I left my kids. I walked away from my life. I left it all behind for him. Why? Honestly? I have no idea. Maybe this will help you, and me, to understand.

It doesn't matter any more. An end is coming. I can't stop it, the damage was too great, the pain too large. You asked me what happened, but I couldn't tell you. Then when I was ready to speak it was too late.

The Portals are sealed now and there's no way I can find of getting back to you. I broke it all, again, and I'm sorry.

I sit here at my desk and I write longhand by the flickering light of an oil lamp. I have freshly-cut quills and reed pens and ink made especially for me. But it wasn't made for this. It was made to indulge me. I like to write things down where the ink makers like to recall their history aurally. There is no electricity here and no computers. My life is simple in its complexity and I can't trust that this peace will last. It's all gone so horribly wrong. I don't know how to make it right.

Shall we start at the beginning then? It does really depend on where you decide it started I suppose. Does it start with my birth? I suppose it could, but then it would be a very long and very boring tale to tell and to listen to, or read. It could start the day Kate walked into my class at school, maybe the day I had sex for the first time, the day I gave birth. It could start at any point in my life. But it is really a culmination of all those and other times and places which made me who I am today. They all focused, all came together one dark autumn night a couple of years ago.

I'd told you I was going to see my parents. Of course I meant my adoptive parents. It was late October. The leaves were golden, red and orange as they tumbled from the trees into drifts on the pavements and blew all over the town centre. It was a day or two before Hallowe'en, Samhain, that night of changes. It was cold, wet and dark.

I had planned to spend a day or two with my parents. I had wanted to ask them so much. I'd only just found out about being abandoned as a baby. In thirty-one years they had never mentioned anything about my being adopted.

I got in my dented green car and set out but the anger was too much, the confusion too great. I couldn't concentrate on driving. So after a couple of near misses and misjudgements I decided to stop. I pulled into the woods to calm myself a bit. I sat there and watched the clouds get heavier and darker, casting a deep gloom over the trees and deepening the shadows. So empty inside.

I sat and watched the sun go down and the moon rise, not that I could see much through the clouds and the rain running down the glass in front of me. I sat there and thought as the rain got steadily heavier until my vision was obscured by the rivulets of water cascading down. A churning numbness filled the pit of my stomach as my mind whirled around a myriad of possibilities. "What if..." can be such a dangerous game to play at any point in your life but this was the worst possible time.

I had stumbled on the adoption documents while clearing out an old dusty cupboard at my parents' house. An old yellowed envelope caught my eye, brittle at the edges with age and stuffed full of papers. Amongst these were the adoption documents naming me and my adoptive parents. There was also a bundle of old, crispy newspaper clippings that told of a decent-sized, healthy newborn baby girl who had been left on the steps of the hospital. The baby had been wrapped in a green, handmade, woollen blanket and was a few days old at most. A number of appeals for the mother to come forward had been made. The clippings spoke of her need to at least seek medical attention. They had all proved fruitless. The last clipping was dated only a couple of months after the first. They hadn't tried that hard.

They didn't know I'd found it all yet, I hadn't told anyone. I'd gone home and stewed, growing more and more irritable and argumentative. I needed to sort this out and fast.

All I'd told you was that I needed to go and see my parents without my kids, that there was something personal and serious to discuss. You, bless you, hadn't questioned me, you'd just agreed to look after my children for as long as it took. It was half-term; they'd be fine for a day or two. I knew that when I got there it would be at least an overnight discussion. It would take time to sort out this tangle.

"Come back when you're ready," you'd said. I knew you meant it but I hadn't planned to be gone longer than overnight. I was angry though, angry enough to lash out and hurt my parents. They didn't deserve that. They'd been good to me, put up with my teenage years, even understood when I got pregnant and refused to tell them who the father was. Not that it mattered. Then when I did it again, they understood that too. They were more parents to me than any woman who had happened to give birth to and abandon me.

But I was still angry, still very confused and hurt. So I'd come to the woods to calm down. I wanted to talk to them, not shout and scream. I wanted to know why they hadn't told me. I was thirty-one and had children of my own now. I should have been told. How could I be the person I was? I felt like I had lived a lie all my life. So I sat there and kept the engine running so I could have the heaters on.

The moon was very full and so bright I could see her through the clouds. It was cold outside but the car stayed warm. The windows were steaming up but I didn't wipe them, there was nothing to see outside but rain and trees. The woods were a place I'd always gone to think and be quiet, ever since I could remember. I'd spent a lot of my teenage years here, but not sitting in a car. I'd built a shelter once but it got pulled down. I'd been soaked to the skin, got blue with cold and had sex for the first time, all in these woods. They were a safe place for me, a place where life-turning events got pondered and worked out in my head. I had parked as close to the old oak as I could get. I'd always loved that tree. It was so big, so old and just, well, magical. It was like the apple tree in the first Narnia book. Do you remember that? The tree that grew from the apple?

As a child I was sure this oak tree should show me the way to another world, another life. As a teenager I had sat beneath its branches and dreamed of being taken away from my life, dreamed of a fantasy existence somewhere else. Little did I realise. How could I have known?

Earlier that day I had spent the afternoon with you, my best friend since school. Best friends and as inseparable as we'd been since when we first met when you walked into the classroom. You and I had done our usual tea drinking marathon and made our way steadily through a whole packet of biscuits while we chattered on about nothing. I'd intended to tell you about the adoption papers, I wanted to tell you, but I couldn't. I don't know why. I'd normally tell you anything. You, on the other hand, took everything to Lily now, or Jack.

Lily. There were times when I thought I knew her and then she'd surprise me again and she was a stranger. So many secrets.

My mind wandered around our friendships and how they had changed over the years as I gazed at the fogging on the inside of the car windows. I wiped a sleeve over it but it just smeared and made it worse so I gave up. I had my mobile on the seat next to me and three or four times I picked it up but there was no signal. There never was in those woods. I left it on and shoved it into my jacket pocket. My fingers brushed against a box of matches already in there. I'd taken them from Susan that afternoon. For a three year old she was daft about fire. She had always loved candles and bonfires. Tom was more wary. He'd stay back and look from a distance. But Susan? She'd get as close as she could. That afternoon I'd caught her striking matches and watching the flame eat the wood. I was the same as a child. I'd sit for hours watching the patterns in the fire. I used to make up stories while I sat there. My parents said I was away with the fairies. I must admit that when I was day-dreaming like that I wasn't aware of anything around me. Aren't most kids like that though? So, I'd taken the matches from my daughter and stuck them in my pocket. There they still sat. I took the box from my pocket and shoved a thumb in one end to push the little drawer out. There were still plenty left she couldn't have had them long. Cold tightness squeezed at my guts. It would only have taken one dropped-and-still-lit match to set a fire in her bedroom. My eyes closed against the possibility.

Not for the first time that day, I caught myself wondering what my children would do without me. That was why I'd made you and Jack legal guardians of them and made a living will stating that if anything were to happen then you should have care of the children. I didn't want my parents adopting another generation. Not my kids. And not until I had it all worked out.

I had a box of matches in my hand, a car full of petrol and a hopeless feeling deep inside. I came so close at that moment.

I let my thoughts explore the various reasons my parents hadn't told me I was adopted. Was it because there was some big secret about my mother they'd found out? Did they think I'd react badly? Well, this was worse. The hurt ran incredibly deep, soul deep, through every fibre of my being.

I was startled out of my reverie by a tap on the car window, right by my head. Heart suddenly racing I snapped my head round to see a shadowy figure leaning on the car. A muffled voice asked something but I couldn't make out the words. Hesitantly I opened the window a crack. The rain poured down his hair and face. He asked me if I was OK and what I was doing in the woods that late. I was a bit taken aback by that until I looked at my watch. It was midnight.

He was tall, over six feet, and solidly built. Broad shoulders tapered into the narrowest waist I'd seen on a man. He looked like he spent his life in the gym, or worked out every day. Firmly muscled arms pushed at the fabric of his jacket and his powerful chest pulled at the buttons of his shirt as he breathed. His hair dripped water onto his shoulders but he didn't seem to notice. His hair was dark, probably black but I couldn't see well enough to be sure. It curled in a tight cascade down to brush the tops of his shoulders and was tucked behind his ears. A neat beard and moustache lined his smiling mouth. His eyes were dark, as dark as his hair, but they blazed with something not quite of this world. His arms were raised as he rested his hands on the roof of my car. He smiled at me and his arms fell away from the car to rest limp at his sides. I found myself winding the window down a little further. He was an imposing figure but I felt oddly safe. I was alone, in the dark, in the rain, in the woods and there was a strange man leaning on my car. I'd seen enough horror films, it was a classic scene. I should have wound up the windows, locked the doors and driven off. But we know I didn't do that. I did wind the window up but only because the rain was coming in. I felt compelled to talk more with him. He was friendly, he seemed to care I was out there and obviously upset. I hadn't seen him around before but he did seem familiar. It was an odd feeling, like my head was a bit foggy. He was incredibly charismatic. So I found myself asking him to sit in the car with me so we could talk in the dry. I know, you'd think that was stupid. I do too, I do now anyway. But I did it. He walked round and got into my car. His weight made the car rock as he climbed in and it shook as he pulled the door closed. Somehow, with him in the car I felt warmer but I left the engine running and the heater blowing warm air over us both.

He didn't try anything. Let me make that clear at the start. We just talked. He didn't tell me his name, nor did he ask me for mine. Not that I remember anyway.

"I was walking in the woods when I saw you." His rich, deep voice resonated through the car. "You seemed sad, distressed even. I was concerned for you, alone here in the dark."

"The dark doesn't worry me," I told him. It never had. Since my teenage years I had considered myself naturally nocturnal.

"Perhaps it should," he suggested. "There are shadows to be found in the dark." It was an odd expression but although I raised an eyebrow at him, he didn't elaborate and it made a weird sort of sense. I shrugged at him and he flashed that dazzling smile again. His eyes sparkled when he smiled. His hands were cradled in his lap, held neatly. They were big hands, not that hairy and not smooth, the hands of a man who knew about hard work. Mainly he sat there quietly and listened as I told him of my discovery and my feelings. Maybe the fact that I was being so open with a complete stranger should have set my internal alarm bells ringing, but it didn't. I felt like I'd known him forever. Now, looking back, I imagine that was the magic.

I had no idea. I didn't even believe magic was real. All I saw was a charismatic man who wanted to listen to me at the exact moment I needed someone to talk to. He spoke when I faltered, he smiled and nodded. He was a good listener. We talked as the moon rose higher, until she was shining right overhead. Or so it seemed. The clouds broke and stars started to show through. The rain slowed to a drizzle and then eventually stopped completely. It was freezing cold and I could smell that metal tang of frost in the air. The leaves under the trees would crunch with ice in the early morning.

"I love the stars," he said "My father used to sit outside with me and tell me stories about the constellations. My favourite was always Orion." I asked him which one that was, I had no clue. I'd never been bothered with constellations although the stars had always brought a smile to my face. There was always something wonderful about a clear starlit night. A full moon made it even more spectacular. His hand rose to point out the belt in Orion and then the arms and legs. He told me of how the great hunter had slain the giant bull. He showed me Orion's enormous bow and his faithful hunting dogs. He spoke of how the hunter had been entrapped by the daughter of the chieftain and that after she'd had her way with him; her father had cast a magical blindness upon him. Orion had fallen into a deep sleep as the enchantment was cast but when he awoke without his sight he was not defeated. Instead he journeyed to the edge of the world and turned his face to the first rays of a new sun, which restored his sight. But he recalled the woman who had trapped him and he fled from her, from his homeland. He left his family and made a home elsewhere. There he fell in love with a huntress almost as great as he was. Blinded by her love for him the huntress was tricked into killing him. After his death, Orion was granted a place in the heavens and his faithful dogs followed him there.

"His story was told to me many times." His voice rumbled hypnotically. "As a child I loved it and demanded it over and over." He smiled again, remembering happy times.

"I can see why," I told him. "It's a classic mythical tale. You told it beautifully. Thank you for sharing it with me. I've never heard the full Orion tale before."

He laughed at me. "You people. You live in this world and yet you never see it. It should be a beautiful, vibrant thing, swelling with life and energy. Yet you hide from it in your dead stone houses and you never see the life around you." I looked at him sideways. His choice of words had set me on edge a bit but he stared at the stars through my windscreen and my wariness melted away like butter in the sun.

"We do." I heard myself agree with him. "The earth deserves more respect but we're not close enough to feel her any more. It's not right but with so many of us and the technology we rely on, there's really no other way. People like to live in a solid, safe structure. We've come to rely on material possessions and, as a result, we like to keep them somewhere." He nodded, agreeing.

"Feeling without roots is a soul-destroying thing." He spoke softly, changing the subject back to my own troubles. "To not know the line from whence you came is a hurtful thing to have kept from you. I am angered on your behalf." He sat there in the passenger seat of my car and summed up how I felt in a few words. He consolidated all my ranting to myself into those phrases, softly spoken as the moon shone down on us. Orion hung in the sky as bright as if he'd just been placed there. "You will always wonder who your mother was and why she left you. She will be your true roots, Sam." I startled at his use of my name, I didn't remember giving it to him. I assumed I must have done and yet I still had no idea of his name. "There is a saying where I was raised." He carried on as if I'd not reacted. "You will always know who your mother is; your father is the man who raised you. We grow within our mother's body. She nurtures us while we are helpless. She cares for us and helps us grow strong. She teaches us the basics of who we are. The mother is the key to each of us. Our mothers and sisters are the foundation of our lives and of our society. They are the soil we fix our roots in and grow from." His words were eloquent and he made sense. They spoke to a deep part of me, to my soul I suppose. They reached my unknown roots and drenched them.

But he only stoked the anger I felt at being abandoned and then lied to for my whole life.

I'd promised to be back in time for Samhain. I shivered. I wished I'd finished knitting my thick jumper. I could see it in my mind's eye, set across the back of the armchair in my living room. I had a sleeve to finish and then to sew it up. Ah well, it couldn't be helped now. I reached out and turned the heater up a notch. I tucked my hands into my sleeves and hugged myself.

"You're cold?" he asked.

I nodded and shivered again. "I should be going really. I have somewhere I should be." I didn't really want to go and have that conversation. I needed to know but I dreaded the tears, the hurt it would cause.

"Should?" He raised an eyebrow in query. "You don't wish to go?"

"I have to go," I told him. "I need to go and sort this out. I need some answers." My protest was only really half-hearted to be honest. While I had been angry I would have stormed to their door and demanded answers. But now, calmer, I wasn't sure what I wanted.

He shook his head and his long curly hair rippled. "You don't have to do anything. You feel obliged to them for your raising. But you don't have to do this." I looked at him quizzically and he paused for a moment before he spoke again, as if gauging my reaction. "It's a choice. You choose to owe them your loyalty just as you can choose to walk away. You choose to want to do this thing, just as you can choose not to do it. It's up to you to decide how much this information is a betrayal, how much it means to you. It's up to you if you want to pursue your mother and find out who she was, who she is, why she behaved as she did. That path can be followed but it leads into the unknown." Again his eloquence struck a chord in me. He was warm and comforting as he sat there next to me in my car. He was strong and a reassuring presence. I should have been so much more wary. I should have never opened the door. I should never have listened to him. But hindsight is a wonderfully clear thing; it is always in crystal clear focus isn't it. If I'd known what was to come I would have done things differently, or so I like to think. Maybe I would have done exactly the same.

Despite what I should have done, when he reached out a hand, I took it. He gazed deep into my eyes and I was lost. He murmured that I was beautiful, that I deserved better than the life I was living. Yet, even then I was not afraid, I was not even wary. I missed the subtle gestures he must have made. I was oblivious to the magic working through me. I was fogged and distracted by him, by his charisma, by his charm. When he spoke, the words sank deep into the core of me. I believed every word he said then. I believed it like I believed the sun would rise in the morning.

"I would show you places and times such as you cannot imagine." His voice purred rather than growled, although it was a deep sound much like you'd imagine a lion making. "I could open doors for you. I could make you Mistress of a Realm beyond this. For you I would do this, I would choose to do this." I sat there; stunned that anyone would say such things to me. The glamour he cast made me unable to see the flaws in his offer, unable to question it. My throat closed and I was unable to speak. "I'm sorry. I presume too much," He apologised.

"No, it's fine." I found myself defending him, reassuring him. "You just took me by surprise. Don't worry about it."

"Then you will forgive me for being blunt?" he asked.

"Of course." I readily agreed.

"I have watched you from afar for a time now." His admission explained the growing feeling of familiarity I felt instead of awakening my caution as it should have done. "I have watched your life unfold and I have felt a wonder at it. Only tonight was I able to step through and come to you as I should have before."

I am no romantic; my view of the world is jaded. I was a strictly one-step-at-a-time kind of girl. Where was that Sam when I needed her caution, her wariness, her reluctance to get involved with anyone? The feeling of strangeness washed over me fleetingly and then was gone, forgotten. His hand was warm and strong around mine. His face smiled gently at me and the world ceased to exist for me. Everything shrank into that one moment, that tiny space inside the car. Nothing else mattered.

So when his hands moved and the light flared I sat and watched.

His hand left mine and he cupped his palms together. His long fingers made a cradle for the tiny spark that formed there. He balanced it in one palm while his free hand flicked fingers around it in a series of complex gestures. His gaze never left my face. A smile eased the corners of his mouth. I wasn't cold any more. The spark grew and the light swirled and glowed warmly. Within the chaos cupped in his hand there formed a world. He showed me a place with no roads, no buildings. I saw a place unspoiled by people, a place of trees and of green grass. I watched as the breeze gently rustled the branches and rippled the grass. The sun shone there, warm and soft.

Abruptly he closed his hand over the image and it was gone. "It is real," he whispered. "I can take you there." He flung open the car door and stepped out, closing it behind him. He left me there, sitting in my car with the engine running. I could have driven away.

I opened the door and stepped out. I leaned on the roof and I looked around for him. The car vibrated under my hands. He stood with his back to me, facing the old oak. I moved to stand at his shoulder. His face was rapt and he glanced sideways at me. His hands moved in a series of motions. He seemed to pluck threads from the air, moonbeams from the sky and he drew energy from the woods around us. The trees seemed to darken as the light flashed from his fingers to coalesce on the oak tree's trunk. The glow widened and brightened until I could barely stand to look at it. It slowly grew and stabilised but was fixed to the trunk. I walked around the tree but the far side was dark.

"A Portal," He breathed. "A Portal to my world. Will you come?" He stepped towards it and turned back. He held out a hand, palm up, inviting me to take it and follow him. My heart stood still.

I took his hand and I stepped through the Portal. I had no idea where I was going and I didn't care.

*Kate reached out and absently picked up the mug siting near her hand. She sipped at it carefully and was surprised to find it warm rather than hot.*

*"Fresh one?" Lily's gentle tones came from behind her, making Kate jump.*

*"Oh, Lily, I'm sorry, I forgot you were here," Kate apologised. "I didn't mean to start reading it right now. I just opened it and, well, you know how it is." She shrugged. Lily nodded, busying herself filling the kettle again. Kate drank down her lukewarm tea and took her mug over to join Lily. "You're right; it's an account of what happened while she was gone that first time. It's going to be hard to read isn't it?" Kate murmured quietly.*

*"I imagine so," Lily agreed, reaching out an arm to hug Kate, who leaned her head on her friend's shoulder before pulling away again.*

*"The kids will be home soon." Kate rummaged about in the fridge. "They'll need some dinner, and so will Jack." The kettle boiled and Lily made fresh tea.*

*"We can sit and drink this first." Lily steered Kate back to her chair and pushed her to sit down. "Then I'll go home and leave you to it." Kate smiled, allowing herself to be ordered about. Lily sat with her and they listened to the clock ticking on the wall until the first two of four tired children arrived, chattering, at the back door.*

# 2. Living

    *Kate sat on her saggy green sofa with a mug of hot chocolate in one hand and the sheaf of paper in the other. She sipped slowly at the steaming drink while never tearing her eyes from the lines of carefully, but not neatly, inked handwriting. The floor near the living room door creaked under the weight of someone entering the dimly lit room.*

    *"You shouldn't be reading in the dark like that," Jack admonished gently and he flicked the main light switch, flooding the room with light. Kate blinked and her eyes flicked up at him as she scowled her disagreement. Jack grinned at her expression and*

*stepped into the room. "I'm serious," He laughed. "You'll damage your eyes." He walked over and sat beside her. "What's that?" He waved a hand towards the papers. The same hand and arm he draped affectionately over her shoulder. Kate shrugged him off.*

*"It's something Lily brought for me to read," she answered evasively, unwilling to share that part of Sam with him. She slid the papers down the side of the sofa and leaned on Jack as she finished her hot chocolate.*

I stepped into that light. I left my car with its engine running in the woods without a second thought. I took his warm hand and I let him lead me through into another world.

The air grew thicker and the light surrounded us as we walked through. It was an odd sensation, walking on light, after squelching through the leaf litter in the woods. We reached a point where all I could see was the light coruscating around us. I could no longer see my world and I wasn't sure which direction it was in. Had I chosen to flee just then I would have had no idea which direction to run in.

His hand was firm and reassuring, wrapped around mine. "Stay close," he instructed me, but in a kind way. It was only a few steps but time stood still in there. There was nothing. There was no up or down, no left or right. Nothing was solid. It was weird. My heart raced as I took my first steps into the unknown. I had no idea where we were going but he seemed to know the way so I meekly followed along.

After a while the light shimmered into a think fog and we stepped through that onto soft springy grass. We stood in a glade surrounded by trees. The air was clean and smelled of earth and greenery.

"My home," he said. His words were laden with meaning. When he said home he meant the whole forest. He implied a deep connection, an intrinsic belonging. He stood tall and proud, breathing in the refreshing air. He didn't let go of my hand as he turned and waved his other hand at the light still shining behind us.

It shrank down to a point and flickered from existence. I knew a brief moment of panic then. He had just closed my route home as easily as he had opened it. It not only closed, it vanished. There was no sign it had ever existed.

"How did you do that?" I asked him as I stared at the grass where the gateway of light had been only seconds before. I blinked as if that might bring it back. He grinned at me and tugged at my hand so I had to follow him. We walked hand-in-hand for what seemed like hours. As we walked, he talked.

"These trees have grown here since before my father's father was born." His other hand flung out in expansive gestures as he pointed things out. The day was bright and warm in complete contrast to the cold, dark and wet we had left. Only as I felt the sun's gentle warmth on my back did I realise quite how cold I had been while I sat in the car. My toes tingled as they thawed out, as did my fingertips. I also became aware I was hungry and thirsty, as well as tired. My sense of time had drifted off with the abrupt change in light and season.

So I happily clung to him as a source of solidity, as a rock in a shifting world. I suspect now that was his intention. Still, it was lovely to walk through the trees and feel the sun on my back.

Dappled light spread patterns across the forest floor, rippling as the trees swayed in the cool, but gentle, breeze. I started to pay more attention to my surroundings. The trees were richly coloured in reds and gold. Their leaves hadn't started to drop yet but it wouldn't be long. I reached out a hand to drag fingers through the dry leaves hanging from a large maple. The branches reached down to brush the top of my head. He paused to let me explore the tree.

"Would you like to rest a while?" he asked softly. "I sense you are weary." I smiled at him and nodded. I was like a trusting child and he was the grown up. We found a space on the grass where the sun warmed and dried it. The grass was soft and springy and the warmth relaxed me, although my stomach growled with my growing hunger. He smiled at the sound and asked me to stay where I was. He vanished into the trees without another word and

was lost to my sight in moments. I sat and hugged r
took a long look around me. By now I wasn't sure o
to the glade where the gateway had opened. I wond
fixed thing or whether he could open the gateway a
seemed to have been focused on the oak tree trunk a
but there was no physical object to fix it onto in the glade. I leaned
my head back and gazed up at the golden red of the maple above
me. With the sun shining behind the leaves it looked almost as if
the tree was on fire. I was captured by the sheer natural beauty of
it, towering majestically above my head.

 I slowly became aware of noises around me, normal woodland
sounds. There were birds singing sweetly somewhere and insects
buzzed. The wind softly eased the branches against one another,
making an easy shushing sound. Soothed by the background noise I
didn't hear him return.

 Back at my car, his clothes hadn't seemed out of the ordinary.
Even after stepping through the gateway I hadn't paid that much
attention to them. But as he stepped from the trees I noticed they
were more rough than the memory I held in my mind. Perhaps the
light was making me see it differently. Now I looked closer his
clothing seemed hand-stitched and a rougher weave of fabric than I
remembered. He moved with the grace of a man at home in his
surroundings and he carried an armful of wood topped with a dead
rabbit. In his other hand he carried his jacket, which was being
used as a basket. Grinning, he dropped all this at my feet. He let the
jacket fall open revealing smaller pieces of wood, a pile of berries
and mushrooms of various sorts.

 He kicked the grass away from a patch of earth and built a fire,
pulling flint and steel from his pocket and striking a spark like it
was an everyday occurrence. Within moments he had a small blaze
burning. Then he pulled a short, but wickedly sharp, knife from his
boot and proceeded to skin and gut the rabbit. Using some of the
longer, sturdier sticks he rigged up a rough spit and began to roast
the rabbit. He pulled out the larger mushrooms and brushed the soil
off them. Then he trimmed them a little before setting them back

jacket. He handed me a leaf full of berries, mostly ckberries. They were sweet and delicious. The juice in them slaked my thirst somewhat but didn't resolve it completely.

"We can find fresh water a short distance from here," He remarked as he turned the rabbit to prevent it charring. "This is rough fare but it will sustain us for the walk we have ahead. It is not far but you are tired." He smiled in reassurance and gave me the rest of the berries. He wasn't eating and I commented on that to him. He told me he had eaten just before we met and he could wait until we reached his home where there would be a feast fit for my station. He turned the rabbit again and balanced the mushrooms on top. The aroma coming from that small fire was enticing and my mouth was watering. The berries had taken the edge from my hunger but had in no way filled my stomach. As the meat cooked he poked at it with his knife, making sure it was cooking all the way through. Eventually, after what seemed like an age he proclaimed it ready and drew it from the fire, carefully tipping the mushrooms from the top onto my leaf plate.

"In my home there are plates and knives, proper cooking fires and ovens. There can be fine breads baked fresh daily, sweets such as you will never have have tasted before." He told me these things as he used his knife to slice up the rabbit and hand me slices of steaming hot meat. "But I like to be able to do the simple things too. I like to know I will survive if the situation ever arose. I do not like someone else to be able to do something I cannot." There was a fierce pride in his voice. The rabbit meat was gamey and not that tender but it was hot, cooked and tasty. It was also incredibly greasy. The mushrooms were lightly roasted and oozing with juice. They were delicious.

His laughter made me look up at him. "You are dripping meat grease all down you." He pointed and sure enough, I was. "I will arrange for new clothes for you when we arrive. Don't worry about it for now." I blushed. I could feel the heat rising in my cheeks. His hand came to sit on top of mine, gentle for such a big hand. "I said it is fine. Don't worry. Your clothes can be cleaned and I will make sure you do not need to be naked while that happens." My blush deepened at the thought of that. I couldn't meet his eye, even though I heard the humour in his voice. He waited for me to eat as much as I wanted and then he rose, kicked over the fire and stamped about making sure the last embers were fully extinguished. I rose to join him. Despite the sun, I felt a cold dampness in my clothes from sitting on the ground and my hips ached. I rolled them to ease the rising stiffness.

We walked until the sun dipped into the trees and the walking eased the stiffness in my back and hips. I was tired by the time we reached his home. I stood at the edge of a meadow filled with golden autumn grasses and littered with poppies like blood drops. Ahead of me was the most imposing structure. The meadow grew right up to the foot of a sheer cliff of dark stone. Carved into the rock was a fortress. It couldn't have been made to be anything but defensive. The weight of eons hung on the cliff face. It loomed above me so I had to crane my neck to see the top. The joins between the natural rock and the carved and structured parts were seamless. Stone flowed into shaped walls, door and windows. In the centre there stood a massive iron bound double door you could have driven a car, or ridden a horse through. It was ugly, dark and more than a little bit scary. He took my hand again and led me across the meadow, pausing once to pull a selection of the flowers that grew in amongst the knee-high grasses. He handed me a fistful of random flowers with a smile. It was such a spontaneous thing for him to do I was taken aback.

We must have been observed approaching because, as we got closer, the huge doors eased open silently and the gaping entrance stood before us. As he took me in he waved a hand in a seemingly random manner. But along the walls ethereal light blossomed and suddenly it was no longer dark inside. He pulled me further in, calling instructions as we went. Voices from other areas answered him and I knew that good food, drink and clothing would be with us shortly. It wasn't long before we entered a room that was astounding in its sumptuous opulence. The ceiling was high and lit with tiny lights that made it look like a night sky. The walls were clad in pale wood and hung with tapestries. Thick rugs lined the floor. A large fire blazed in the hearth and a screen to one side offered the promise of a hot bath. The chairs at the table were thickly padded and looked extremely comfortable. The table was already littered with a couple of bottles, glasses and bowls of fruit and obviously-hot bread.

"Please, make yourself at home." He opened his arm to usher me into the room. He followed me in and drew back the screens to reveal a tub of steaming and fragrant water liberally sprinkled with flower petals. I remember laughing at him, at the whole situation then. Only a few hours before I had been dreaming of living a fantasy life and now here it was. I had the vague feeling that perhaps I would wake up in a moment, cold and cramped in the car. He picked up one of the bottles and sniffed at it appreciatively. "Excellent," he murmured "Mulled wine, it will warm you." He poured a glass and handed it to me, it did smell lovely. A tap at the door made us both turn. There stood a man bearing a pile of clothing.

"It is the best we have at the moment Master Ametsam." The man gave a small bow. "More will be ready by tomorrow afternoon if we could have the lady's measurements?" At the top of the pile were several fluffy looking towels. I wasn't sure if Ametsam was his name or a title. But, whoever he was, he took the pile from the man at the door and placed it carefully on one of the chairs. He took the towels and hung them on the screen where they could catch the warmth from the fire. Then he suggested I might like to use the scented water. He nodded his head to me and left, closing the door behind him. The water was hot and smelled divine. The clothing chosen was sort of medieval in style and draped on me like nothing I had ever worn before. When I was out of the bath and dressed again Ametsam reappeared. He brought a handful of people with him, all bearing platters and pots of food. I felt like a princess in a fairytale. So it began. That was my first night with him. I was fed good food and plied with mulled wine until I was falling asleep. Then I was shown into an adjoining room where there was a child's dream of a bed. It was huge and piled with a quilted throw, beneath which were blankets. The pillows were soft and I sank onto them gratefully. I felt him lift my legs under the covers and he whispered in my ear that it didn't matter how long I stayed, that only a few days would pass at home. I barely registered his words as I fell asleep but I heard him leave the room and the door close.

That was how my life there began. It was gentle and welcoming. Ametsam was his name, not a title and he was referred to as the Master of the Realm. He was courteous and kind. He constantly assured me that little time would pass in my own world and I could stay with him for as long as I wished. So I stayed. I was besotted with him.

The following morning I awoke to find him sitting on the edge of the bed. I could smell fresh bread and something else I couldn't identify. He brought me fresh hot water for washing and another clean dress. Then he left me to deal with it all myself. I was glad of the privacy to be honest. I pulled the soft green linen dress over my head and grinned at myself. There was a mirror in the room and I admit I spent a few minutes posing in front of it. It was most unlike me but the way he was behaving and the surroundings had gone to my head a bit I suspect. I had never thought of myself as attractive, certainly not beautiful. Yet Ametsam with his quiet assurances and gentle manners made me feel beautiful. Those early times were special. I basked in the attention I was getting. Those rooms were mine alone. He let me rearrange them, change things as I wished.

My days were filled with adventure. We walked out amongst the trees and he taught me their names. He did it in a way that felt like the trees were somehow more alive than I expected. He spoke to the trees as if they could understand him.

One morning I woke to hear a bustling in the corridor outside my room. When I got up I found a pot of water warming by the fire. Someone always made sure the fire stayed alight in my rooms. There was always a full basket of wood and a blaze in the hearth. I poked at the fire a little and threw an extra log on. The fire roared into life and the washing water was soon warm. I washed and dressed as usual and was surprised to find a lavish breakfast already laid out on my table. There was fresh bread laden with seeds and fruit, a pot of honey, a crock of yellow butter and a bowl of late seasonal fruits. A covered pot by the fire was full of hot porridge. As always there was more than enough for me, more than enough for one person. Maybe they thought Ametsam shared my breakfasts as he shared all other meals with me. Our routine had settled so that on most days he appeared about mid morning and we spent the day together. Then he left me as I grew tired in the evenings. It was a slow and formal courtship and I almost wished to speed it up.

But this day was different. He didn't come to me before my lunch was brought. The man who brought it was the same one who had brought the clothing on the first night. He brought everything that was needed in my rooms. He never told me his name. Names seemed to be something you didn't tell people. I was referred to as Respected Consort, which had a nice ring to it. I liked the respected part and the consort part seemed to involve being seen with Ametsam on a regular basis. He certainly asked no more than that of me during those first few weeks. Lunch that day was a platter of hot sliced meats, more fresh bread, ripe tasty cheese and a pot of root vegetable soup. I asked him where Ametsam was and he smiled indulgently. Ametsam was making preparations apparently. Preparations for what I had no idea. So I ate alone and wondered where he was. My life had begun to revolve around him. But I was happy. I had everything I wanted, more than that I had my every wish indulged. If I mentioned I fancied a new dress, one was there in the morning. When I spoke of boredom with the food, the next day it was changed. The morning I said I'd not slept well and the bed was lumpy, that night there was a fresh mattress and new bedding. I admired some flowers I saw growing and the same day a huge bunch was standing in a vase in my rooms. I felt adored. I wasn't used to it. So I revelled in the feeling.

Ametsam came into my rooms just before dusk. He was dressed finely. New tightly fitting leather trousers clung to his muscular legs. New and polished boots came almost to his knees.

A fine linen shirt covered his broad chest and a soft jerkin-style jacket was over that. He made an impressive figure standing there in my doorway. He bore in his arms a beautiful fabric and he was grinning like a child at Christmas. With a flourish he let the fabric unfold from his arms. It slid smoothly to hang from his raised hands, all the way to the floor.

The delicate material draped perfectly and evenly. The symmetry of the dress was breathtaking. It must have been days in the making at least, if not weeks. The deep purple shimmered as it fell. The skirt of the dress flared out from a narrow waist which rose into a fitted bodice. The bodice was laced and beaded in a series of intricate patterns. The neckline was scooped elegantly and the full-length sleeves were set in perfectly. More beadwork adorned the ends of the sleeves. I gasped at the sight. It was the most gorgeous garment I had ever seen.

"Is that for me?" I asked him incredulously. He nodded and held it out to me. I reached out and took it carefully. It weighed next to nothing and threatened to pour through my shaking fingers like water. "May I try it on?" My voice shook.

He stepped into my room and closed the door. "That was the idea." He smiled. "It is Solstice tonight. You will wear this for the celebration." He sat himself in one of my chairs by the fire and he waited. "Go on." He waved me towards the bedroom. "In private if you feel you must, but change into the dress please." He poured himself a glass of wine and then poured a second to wait for me. I retreated to the bedroom and undressed slowly. The purple dress waited for me, casually flung over the bed. A shiver ran over my exposed skin. I picked up the fine purple fabric and pulled it over my head. It sat on my shoulders like it were gossamer. The sleeves clung to my arms and elaborately expanded to flow fabric below my hands without getting in the way. The bodice was a perfect fit and the skirt was a fairytale. It swirled around my legs in an expanse of luxury almost down to my ankles. I stepped out of the room to see Ametsam look round from the fire. The flames danced in his dark eyes and he slowly rose to greet me. Beside his chair was a pair of new, soft leather boots. I sat on his still-warm chair and I pulled them on. The leather was supple and eased onto my feet like a second skin. He offered me his arm and I took it. As we stepped from the rooms I was startled as a pair of armed warriors fell into step behind us.

"It's just ceremonial, don't worry," he murmured as he placed his hand over mine, which rested on his arm. We walked down to the big double doors. They stood wide open and I could see a large unlit bonfire out in the meadow. The sun was dipping towards the tops of the trees and the shadows cast were lengthening. He paused, framing us in the entrance and a roar came from the throng around the heap of wood. The warriors stood at our shoulders. I call them warriors rather than soldiers because Ametsam had always referred to them as his warriors. He never called them soldiers although he clearly commanded them. I had no idea how many there were, different faces came and went. I had only seen human faces before the Solstice bonfire. He hadn't prepared me at all for the creatures that stood before us as we waited there in the doorway. They were so varied, so different that I couldn't identify any from my own mythology. There were no centaurs or fawns, no talking animals. This was no Narnia. That would have been fun. Those had been favourite stories as I grew up.

There were darkly twisted dwarfish creatures. There were green-skinned delicate women and powerfully built men. There were slender androgynous creatures I might have called elven. More of his warriors mingled among them, their weapons polished and gleaming, but sheathed. Each individual was as well-dressed and well-presented as they could be. Ametsam waited until they subsided in their greetings and then he waved a hand in what looked like a benediction of some kind. The crowd parted and a wide clear path was left for us, leading straight to the unlit bonfire. He led me there and stood still for a moment.

"Do not fear," he whispered "I am the same person you already know, regardless of the shape I wear." I was confused but I nodded. He took his hand and arm from me and raised his fists to the departing sun. His voice rang out, silencing the muttering of the gathered crowd. "I am Ametsam!" he cried. "I am Master of the Realm. Yet I have hidden from you. I pull the flame from the retreating sun and I demand that it light this, our fire for the longest night." He extended his fingers and seemed to literally pull the flame from the sun as it sank below the horizon. The flames shot from his fingertips to ignite the fire. As the flames leapt high his voice rang out again. "In this light I choose to reveal my form." In pure melodrama he turned the flames onto himself and vanished in a column of fire. I gasped in shock but he continued speaking. "I have been transformed by the power that runs in my veins. It has changed my very blood." He sounded exultant and I was afraid. No, I was terrified. But I dared not move. I dared not even drag my eyes away from this figure of a man who seemed to be cradled by fire. The flames roared around him but he moved and appeared unharmed. The flames flickered and turned blue, and then they sank into his skin. He somehow absorbed them. I don't know how. I suspect it was all for dramatic effect to be honest. It worked. Every pair of eyes there was fixed on him. When the blinding light died a little and our eyes recovered enough to see him again, he was changed. What stood before me was not a man.

 His head slowly turned to look around the throng. Blue lips slowly curled to reveal sharply pointed teeth in a triumphant smile above a short curled goatee beard. Broad nostrils flared and seemed to be savouring the smell of the fire and the gasped reactions of those seeing him for the first time. The deep midnight-blue skin was lightly scaled around the eyes and mouth. The scales were heavier on the thickly muscled neck that sloped into broad shoulders, disappearing into his shirt. His arms and chest were corded with thick muscle that rippled beneath the scales every time he moved. He still wore his fine linen shirt and soft jerkin but they both strained over the more powerful torso. His legs tapered away from his narrow waist and were only just encased in his tight leather trousers clinging to his powerful legs even more than before. His new boots had split and fallen away from his feet. Feet that were no longer human. His legs ended in a hoof, a cloven hoof. Tight dark curls adorned the lower legs, pouring from beneath the tight leather trousers at mid-calf. The same dark curls wove tightly about his head, and cascaded down his back in waves. His ears rose to a sharp point, each just below a small, sharply pointed, horn.

His gaze was steady as it soaked up every detail of the varied people facing him around the bonfire. He threw his head back and he laughed. "Let the feasting begin," he cried and reaching out a clawed hand he grabbed me; almost pulling me off my feet. I flinched away from him but he pulled me close. He snapped his fingers and music began to play. It swirled around us and swept us into a wild dance. Held firmly and heady with what I had just seen, I danced like I had never danced before. He rumbled in my ear, deep and low. "I am still Ametsam. You are still my Respected Consort." I believed him.

We danced for what felt like hours under the emerging stars and rising moon. Long tables had been brought out and were being piled high with food. When my feet ached and the smell of cooking meat mingled with the smoke from the fire in a tantalising aroma, I begged him to stop so I could eat. He pulled me to the tables and piled a selection of food onto a large plate and he steered me to some rough benches which were set up nearby.

After eating we drank wine and then we danced again. It was dark, cold and magical. Eventually I pleaded I was tired and he took me back inside. All round the meadow there were figures still dancing, playing musical instruments or generally partying. A strong drum had dominated the night and it still thrummed through the earth and shook my feet. I looked back over my shoulder as we crossed the threshold and saw that the sun was just starting to pink the edge of the sky. We'd been up all night. As the sun rose he took me for the first time. He was gentle and unlike any man I had ever known before. We made love only the once that night but it was magnificent. Afterwards I rested, cradled in his arms and eventually I slept. He had claimed me as his own and I was happy to be claimed. He had demanded that the sun return and it had done. He had pulled fire from the sky and transformed himself as the fire consumed the wood on the bonfire. He was incredible.

*Ametsam? Incredible? Kate slowly laid down the papers and blew out a long, disbelieving breath. Her head was whirling with what she had just read.*

*Ametsam, incredible? The same Ametsam who had snatched Hayley, who had tormented Kate, tried to kill Lily. But that Ametsam had been a monster. Was he a man then? Was he a man masquerading as a demon through a magical glamour, or a demon hiding as a man under an illusion? Or, and Kate felt the cold truth of it, had he changed into something evil, just as his son had begun to change and would have continued to change if Susan hadn't taken his magic from him.*

*Shaking her head in baffled confusion, Kate carefully patted the papers back into order and slipped them into a slim card folder. This she slid between two large books on the shelf of cookery and gardening books above the fridge.*

# 3. Rules

 

 

The two women sat in the small café and each cradled a steaming mug.

"Did you read it?" Kate asked.

Lily shook her head. "Not all of it," she reassured as she studied the racing thoughts visible on Kate's face. "There's something troubling you?" Kate picked up her mug and breathed in the steam before sipping carefully. Music softly filled the background, filtering from the radio behind the counter. Kate sat and stared into her mug. She set it down.

*"Lily," she began "You knew Ametsam. You lived with him."* Lily nodded, saying nothing, waiting. *"Why? How? When I met him he was evil, a monster. He was a complete bastard. How could you love him? Sam writes about him as if he was the best thing that ever happened to her."* She refused to meet Lily's eyes. *"I'm reading a bloody love story but I know how it ended. I don't understand. I just don't get it."* Kate finally looked up and Lily saw tears.

*"It's complicated,"* Lily explained with a small shrug. *"He was incredibly charismatic and he used his magic in subtle ways to control and dominate."* She took Kate's hand and their eyes met, green and icy blue. *"Kate, we both know how the story ends. This is your chance to find out how it started for Sam."*

After that first time he came to me most nights and I was willing. I was drowning in the attention he lavished on me. The gifts didn't stop once he had claimed me as his own and as his consort. The greatest gift he gave me was his time and his undivided attention. On a few occasions as we walked out on the meadow he was interrupted by a warrior asking for instructions or offering him information. Without fail Ametsam's response was: "Not now, can you not see I am with my Consort? Leave us." Every time, the interrupter backed away with an apology. He was obviously in complete control of his domain and the people in it. I hardly ever saw him use his magic. Since opening the gateway, that he'd called a Portal, the only time I had seen the magic being used with a visible effect was at the bonfire. I'm sure he used it daily but in more subtle ways.

He liked to know where I was, where I had been and what I had been doing when he wasn't with me and I was happy to chatter on about my day like it was the most important information in the world to him. We spent many evenings sitting by my fire, in my comfortably padded chairs. I talked and he listened.

He had been right. His transformation had not really changed anything but his appearance. Well, maybe that night had altered the intensity of our relationship, taken it to another level. But it wasn't the physical change. He was still the attentive Ametsam I had known before.

I will admit it was disconcerting to sit drinking herb and fruit teas, or wine, with a man who looked more like the human myth of a traditional devil. One evening I told him so.

"I wore the human form for a time as the change in my own body was completed." He laughed as he explained. "I am no devil, but I thought you would be afraid of my new form. I knew my own people would be unnerved by it until it was finished. I have known people from your world before and they are always afraid of what they find here at first. I had no desire to frighten you." His soft words reassured me. Again, he was right; I would have driven off if he'd appeared to me looking like this. Yet I happily sat there and talked with him, night after night. I allowed him access to my body whenever he desired it, which was frequently.

The seasons turned through an entire cycle and the days were once again white and cold. The leaves that had been richly red and gold were now buried beneath the cold blanket of snow. My rooms were warm and dry, the fire blazed constantly. But I was becoming bored. I tried to find the kitchens and talk to those who prepared my food but as I made my way down the corridor, Ametsam appeared and steered me outside to walk in the snow.

My feet were warm in fur-lined boots and I had managed to persuade him that warm trousers were more practical than another dress. He'd said he preferred me to be draped beautifully and to look attractive but I'd had my way. So my warmest trousers were tucked into the tops of my boots. The tunic was definitely designed to flatter a female figure and was adorned with decoration like everything else I owned here. I longed for some simple, plain clothing but my requests fell on deaf ears. I hadn't seen my old clothes since the first night when he'd promised to have them cleaned for me.

As we approached the doorway Ametsam plucked a long woollen cloak from a small room there that I had not noticed before. He pulled it round my shoulders and fastened it with an elaborate cloak pin. There was a full hood and although I pulled it up, he tugged it down again saying he liked to see my face as we talked. So the hood stayed down and my ears froze.

"Sam." He began slowly as if uncertain how to broach the subject. "You know how I love you." He searched my face while I nodded, heart hammering in my chest. "Do you have children? You do not speak of any." I felt a moment of shame. I should have told him. I wasn't sure why I hadn't.

"I do," I replied. "A boy and a girl."

"That is good." He seemed satisfied and didn't press me for more. I told him of Thomas and Susan anyway. I told him of their fathers, I told him they were with a close friend and as long as I got home with only a day or so passing in my world they would be fine. Then he asked me the question I knew would come.

"Would you bear more children if I asked it of you?" his voice was calm and gentle. I looked at him and I nodded slowly.

"I think so," I said "Why? Are you asking me now?" He shook his head. No, he wasn't asking yet but he explained he was in a position where an heir was important and there would be rumours if one wasn't apparent soon.

We walked further. The snow was clean and crisp. The sun sparkled on the loose ice crystals on the surface and shone in the ice hanging from the trees. He didn't seem to feel the cold. My feet started to get that painfully numb that comes in the snow. I pulled the cloak tightly around me and shivered. He kept me walking for a while longer. Or rather I followed him as he carried on walking. We circled through the trees in quiet companionship as I pondered his question about children. I was torn. Could I bear his children? Could I even conceive with him? More importantly did I want a child to bind me here over my existing children? Would he let me fetch them? How would I explain this to you Kate? When was I going to wake up?

Eventually we drew near to the fortress again and he took me inside, directly back to my rooms. Along the way he called out instructions so hot food and drink arrived shortly after we did. He poked up the fire until he had it roaring dangerously and then he took my cloak and boots before bidding me sit by his frighteningly high fire. The heat was wonderful and I saw my trousers begin to steam as they dried.

"Hold on here?" I asked him "I'm going to change into dry clothes." He smiled and opened the door to the man who had been about to knock. I had to smile at him, standing there with one hand raised to tap on the door as it swung open. A platter with a tureen of hot soup, a plate of bread and steaming, fragrant tea was carefully balanced on his other hand. I turned and retreated to my bedroom to change, pulling the door closed behind me. I could hear the food being laid out in the other room and my stomach was certainly ready for something after the walk. I pulled off my wet trousers; the snow had soaked them to the knee. I left the tunic and pulled on dry trousers and socks. I pulled out a sweater I had knitted myself since being here. I was proud of it.

Ametsam frowned as I went back into the main room. "You should dress more appropriately," he told me. "I provide you with appropriate clothing, why do you choose to wear that?" He pointed at my sweater.

"Because it's warm and I'm not," I grumbled. His frown didn't lift but he said no more. But a fine-fur lined cloak was waiting for me a few days later, a sure sign that the sweater was not to be seen again.

That first year was a whirlwind. Oh yes, it was years. He assured me many times that only a few days would pass for you and for my children. He promised me, he gave me his word and I believed him. I believed every word right up until I came home and you told me just how long I had been away. He had me take part in ceremonies. He had me watch the initiation of new warriors. I spent my days at his side. I was his consort. I felt like a queen.

But more and more I felt constrained. His opinions and preferences were becoming more forceful and his suggestions more like orders. The sweater was an example. Shortly after he had expressed his displeasure it vanished. He told me he was sorry but it had been damaged in the cleaning, it was not possible for it to be repaired. When I said I could easily make a new one he laughed and said I had no need to make anything.

I questioned him about it more than once. "Why do I need to wear that dress?" I asked him one day when he had chosen a particular garment for me.

"Because you are my consort," he replied, looking baffled "You are seen with me and must reflect my status. Surely you understood that?" I did in a way. I was in a special position at his side and I felt it. But I didn't understand it. I had only been there a short time and I knew little of the customs and traditions he upheld. So I let him guide me.

On one of my rare wanders around the fortress I stumbled on a wall with some carvings. They could have been pictograms, or patterns, or even writing. I had taken a wrong turn and found myself in a dark, poorly lit corridor grimy with disuse. The floor was thick with dust and cobwebs hung from the ceiling, tangling in my hair and sticking unpleasantly to my clothes.

"You should not have been there." He chastised me when I mentioned them to him. "That place is dangerous, unstable. I will not have you go there again." His manner grew gentler. "Sam, I would not see you hurt. I care too deeply for you. I still hope you will someday bear me a child. I will take no other to be my consort even if it means I have no legitimate heir." His face fell and he turned away. In the face of his obvious distress how could I refuse him?

"Then I will agree to try and conceive your child." I reached out to touch his shoulder and he turned back to me. "Maybe someday I can go and fetch my other children. They would love it here."

He nodded slowly. "Perhaps." He agreed, but I felt his reluctance. "Perhaps someday they can come and be with you." We left it at that. He wanted a child and I wanted my children. I hadn't been using any form of protection and I was wondering why I hadn't become pregnant before then. But it made him happy for me to say I would try. Like I had any real control over when I conceived.

So we started to think about a baby. Every few weeks I would bleed and the chance was gone again. Each time this happened he grew darker and a little more distant. I tried to talk to him.

"Ametsam," I said, cautiously one evening as we sat by my fire. "I had no trouble conceiving before."

He flew into a rage. "So you're blaming me?" he bellowed angrily "It's my fault?" His face was dark with his anger and the muscles on his arms and chest were bunched and swollen. "I have fathered children before. It is no fault of mine." He stormed from the room. I ran to the door and followed him.

"Ametsam!" I called. "That's not what I was going to say." I scurried after him as he walked away, striding down the corridor. "Come back. Please." I could hear the begging in my voice but I didn't care. "Come back with me. Come and sit with me. Let me finish. Ametsam? Please?" He slowed his pace and stopped. He didn't turn to face me. I could see his hands curled into fists at his sides, his arms corded and thick with tense muscle. He lowered his head and a shiver ran over his shoulders. I watched as he fought for self control. Finally he turned.

"Come then," He spat and thrust past me to return to my rooms. He flung the door open with such force that it bounced off the jamb and flew back into my face. I flung up a hand and narrowly avoided an injury. The door was heavy, solid and ancient wood dense with the weight of years. I pushed it open again to find him standing in front of my fire. His arms were folded tightly across his chest. He glowered at me, his dignity affronted. At that moment he looked the part. The tall, cloven hoofed demon standing framed by licking flame. Yet I felt I knew him better. He was no demon, just a man physically changed by his use of magic. He was a man who had just had his masculinity insulted.

"I'm sorry," I began as I entered my rooms. I'm not sure why I apologised but it seemed to placate him a little. "Ametsam, I am truly sorry. You misunderstood me. That's not what I was saying. I have borne children before and you have fathered children. It's not either one of us." He still stood, tightly contained and glowering at me. But he said nothing. He listened as I spoke. "But I am not from your world. You have changed from a man into what you are now. Perhaps we are just not compatible?" It sounded lame, even to me. From the look on his face he wasn't even close to thinking about being convinced. "Ametsam, listen!" I pleaded with him. "We won't stop trying. If it is possible for me to bear you a child then I will. I'm just not sure that our genetics are compatible."

"Genetics?" the foreign word caught his attention as it confused him. "What is genetics?"

I tried to explain. "You know how when animals breed they only breed with their own kind? They only produce their own kind?" He nodded so I carried on. "Trees and flowers take pollen from one flower to make seed in another but only ever make more of themselves. It's nature at its best Ametsam. Like only ever reproduces like. A species replicates itself. Now and then, very rarely a new thing is created but it is incredibly rare. Perhaps we will create that new thing, that new life never seen before. But perhaps we won't." His face was darkening again and his brows furrowed where they had been starting to soften at my words. "Wait!" I called. "It is early days yet. Maybe we don't even need to think about this. Maybe a child will come naturally for us. Maybe it will just take time. We will keep trying."

He relented a little. "Yes, we can do that," he grudgingly admitted. The air was not exactly clear between us and the subject far from closed but a truce had been called. That night he was rampant and rough. But I was more than equal to the task. I don't think either of us got any sleep much before dawn.

After that he was always with me. He arrived in my rooms with my breakfast and stayed to eat with me. Then there was always some business he had to deal with so I was left in my rooms.

I started trying to go for a walk in the mornings but before I'd taken more than a couple of steps outside my door I heard footsteps behind me.

"Respected Consort?" A female voice came from over my shoulder. "I am to accompany you if you wish to go out walking. I am at your command." I turned to see a tall female warrior. She was taller than me and her skin was sun browned to a rich olive. Her straight golden hair was caught back in a long braid adorned with beads at the end. The braid was pulled to one side and hung over her shoulder. Her tough leather trousers were tucked into hard boots. I could see the hilt of a long knife tucked into one boot. As I paused to wait for her she buckled on a belt with a short sword hanging from it. She hastily tucked her shirt in and pulled her jerkin straight. A swift loosening of the sword in its sheath to check it was loose and she was ready. My mind raced as we walked across the meadow into the trees.

"I would like to see more of this land." I tried to engage her "I feel I have seen so little of it. Is there a way of travelling faster here?" Everywhere Ametsam had taken me we had walked. There was no doubting that I was fitter than I had ever been in my life but it was something that had surprised me. I had expected horses or magical teleporting gateways or something.

"The Master has not taken you through the Portals?" She sounded surprised "It is not my place to say. Please forget I spoke." She sealed her lips together and refused to be drawn further. This was something I would have to broach with him. We walked until I was hungry and the sun was high overhead. The trees were beginning to show green at the tips of their new buds. The grass was slowly recovering from being frozen for the past couple of months and although the danger of frost was not yet fully over there were definite signs of growth. The land was coming alive again. My shadow paced alongside me and I got used to having her there. I stopped at the foot of a large, broad-trunked tree and gazed across grass littered with early snow drops. A deeper, broader leaf was spiking through between them and held the hope of bluebells in a few short weeks. The bite of ice in the air cut at my nose and lips while the sun warmed my back. I stood and stared while I wondered if this quickening of the earth would mean that my womb would quicken with his child. I laid a hand flat to my firm stomach and knew it would not be. I had already felt the ache in my back that always came the day before a period. I was aware of my irritability that I knew for PMT. I dreaded telling him we had failed again. I would wait until I began to bleed again, until I was absolutely certain and had proof. I sighed and was aware of her shuffling restlessly behind me. So we slowly walked back to the fortress.

He was waiting in the meadow. He was sparring with one of the larger warriors. Slicked with sweat and naked to the waist, they both shone in the spring sun. Their swords caught the light as they flicked back and forth. Ametsam fought with two blades, as did his opponent. I stopped at the edge of the trees and watched him and I knew he'd seen me. His style didn't change. He was still soundly beating his opponent, driving him back further with each blow. The twin swords whirled around him and I was amazed they never touched each other. The weapons were not padded or wrapped with leather. I hoped they were blunted for practice. The blades hissed past one another with only the thickness of a hair between them as Ametsam wove metal patterns in the air around him.

He crossed his blades while holding them high and he thrust forwards in a single fluid movement. His opponent bent backwards to avoid the scissoring steel and lost his balance, sprawling in the grass. Ametsam grinned as he followed his lunge through to pin the man to the earth with a sword point on either side of his neck. The blades crossed perilously close to his throat but he grinned back up at his Master.

Ametsam tugged the sword points from the earth and one blade pulled against the man's neck, just where it joined the shoulder. From the fine line of red that welled up it was clear that these were not blunted blades. Ametsam smoothly sheathed the clean sword and drew the other blade through the short new growth of grass to clean it before sheathing that one too. Only then did he step away from his victory and offer a hand to haul his opponent to his feet. They spoke briefly and there was clear humour between them before the other man walked briskly back to the fortress. He wiped at his neck and shook his head. His low chuckle could be heard easily across the meadow. Ametsam turned and acknowledged our presence and my shadow left my side, giving me back into his care. He didn't come to me but he beckoned and made me walk to him. He kept his eyes fixed on mine as I walked across the meadow. He held out a dry hand to me as I approached him. The palm was uppermost and it was a clear invitation for me to take it. When I ignored it and made to walk past him he reached out and grasped my hand in a vice like grip. He possessed me with that firm hand hold. He claimed my allegiance and he asserted his control. But I didn't see it. I enjoyed having my hand held. I smiled at the warmth of his hand around mine. I slipped my fingers in between his and laced out hands together more tightly. He pulled me close so I was walking almost on top of him. I leaned into him and he eased his hand free to drape his heavy arm around my shoulders. The sword at his hip bumped into my leg uncomfortably but I didn't care.

He walked me back to my rooms and we shared a meal again. Then we sat and played board games that day. He played dice well and was trying to teach me his favourite version of the warrior's game. There was also a strategy game he had been trying to teach me but I hadn't grasped even the rudiments of it yet. He was a patient instructor and we tried to play every day. He sat at the table, on a chair across from me. The board lay between us. The playing pieces were unfamiliar but the board was like a chessboard, a simple grid. The squares were marked on a wooden board, inlaid panels of light and dark wood. But there the similarity ended.

Where a chess board was eight squares wide this was twelve. A chess board has two colours, a repeating pattern of light and dark, this had three colours. They were marked in a pale yellow wood, a rich red wood and a deep wood that was almost black. The edge of the board was inlaid with geometric parquetry patterns. It was beautifully made and a work of art in itself. The game pieces were individually carved and included a Master, a Mistress and a Keeper on each side. They each led a colour theme within their own ranks. They were protected by law givers and warriors and they in turn were served by a generic piece much like a chess pawn.

I never did get the hang of the game. But I did get my warrior guardswoman to sit with me and carve me a chess set. Somehow she managed to get a board made too and I taught Ametsam to play chess. It didn't confuse him and he was swiftly easily beating me at most games. But my shadow, as I came to call her, was a quick learner too. Many a time I set off for a walk and found her at my side. We often walked on silence and she left a few steps between us so I would feel more alone. But I always knew she was there. Then at the end of the walk she would see me back to my rooms and now and then I managed to ask her in and we played a few games of chess.

I never felt fully alone unless I was asleep and even then most of the time Ametsam was there too.

Then my shadow disappeared. I never really found out what happened but one day she wasn't there. When I asked Ametsam where she had gone his reply was, "Does it matter? I will find you another one." By the end of that day there was a new face at my heels wherever I went.

"Ametsam?" I asked him one day. He turned and raised an eyebrow. "Why do I need someone with me all the time?"

He smiled indulgently. "I worry about you, Sam. You are new to this realm and innocent of its dangers." We were sitting watching a mock battle in the meadow. He took my hand and cradled it between his own larger hands. He shifted in his seat to face me and his dark eyes bored into my grey ones. "Sam, I am not the only user of this magic here. There is another." He hesitated, as if reluctant to say more. We were interrupted briefly by the current battle being won quite decisively. He and I both cheered and applauded the winners as they left the field. The defeated ones groaned and hauled themselves to their feet. They limped and hobbled from the grass and at least one looked to have a broken arm. The fighting hadn't been deadly but wasn't play acting either. As the next battle was lined up and ready to commence he spoke again.

"She is more powerful than I and bears me no good will." His voice was low as if she might hear him. "She was once Mistress here and I was her Consort. She has control over the Portals as I do and she has more strength and subtlety to her power than I. I fear her, Sam." I could read no fear in his earnest expression but then I had always been hopeless at reading other people's body language. I was even confused by my own feelings and found it difficult to put my emotions into words. I stayed quiet and let him speak. "You are my Consort now. I have taken her mantle and made myself Master here. The place you are in, at my side, with no magic of your own is a deadly, dangerous place to be. You are mortal, Sam. You can be harmed or killed here. She will not hesitate to try to harm you. I do not doubt it. So I seek only to protect you." He searched my face for a moment and was obviously satisfied with the concern he saw reflected there. "I had thought I could avoid having to burden you with this but I see it is not possible." I smiled at him then, completely unaware of the delicate manipulation, the subtle misinformation.

I knew who this dangerous woman was. I had eaten at her house. I had drunk tea with her, baked cakes with her. My son regularly played with her son. She had patched up scraped knees and helped with the school run. But he had no way of knowing that and I had no way of knowing that Lily was the dangerous woman of whom he spoke so eloquently. I knew Lily but I didn't link her with the dangerous former Mistress of the Realm. Why would I? Lily was, and still is, my friend, and more. I hope she's told you who she really is to me, to my children, and I hope she is watching over you all for me now. You will all need her strength.

So he framed his rules in two ways. I was relatively new to his Realm and needed teaching. I could accept that. I understood that. I actively encouraged that. I wanted to know so much about the history of his people. I wanted to learn about his magic. I was still fascinated by the pictograms and carvings I found here and there. He needed me to learn about protocols, about traditions. He wanted me to look the part and to act the part. But with no magic of my own that was so incredibly difficult. He explained to me that the Master or Mistress of the Realm usually took a person empowered with the ancestral magic to be their consort. That way any heir born was likely to bear the power too. It also made for a more equal alliance. That made perfect sense to me then.

Now he had presented this perceived threat to my health and even to my life. Not knowing who she was, this woman sounded frighteningly able to deal out any harm she wished. I was afraid, I feared for my life from that moment on. He planted the seeds of fear there and he carefully nurtured them until they threatened to strangle me. But let's not leap ahead.

He spoke of her now and then, his Mistress Lilith of the red hair. He spoke of her anger and of her softness. He told of a woman in complete control of a fierce temper, a woman not to be crossed, a woman who would wreak havoc on a whim. This was a woman who left him abruptly and with no reason. He told me how she had left him in the middle of the night and never returned. He didn't know where she had gone but he had never found her again. He had woken in the morning to find her gone and the Realm without a ruler. Someone had to step up and he was the only one with even a glimmer of the power. So he took on the role and had been Master ever since.

*Kate leaned back in her chair looking pensive. This was starting to paint a different picture and with a sinking feeling she had a hunch she knew where the story was going.*

*But this description of Lily was bizarre. Kate had never seen Lily angry until the days they had spent in her world, finding and rescuing Hayley. Even then Lily had never got truly angry, never out of control like Ametsam seemed to be implying here.* She tipped her chair back and reached for the phone. It rang as her fingers touched it. Smiling she checked the caller display.

"Hi, Lily." Kate smiled, "I was just going to call you." She listened for a moment before answering. "Yes, I'm in. The kids are in bed and Jack's away overnight on a course for work." Another pause as she listened, a grin slowly spreading over her face. "Are you being psychic again? I was going to ask you if we could talk about Sam's thing." Kate laid a hand gently on the papers in front of her. "Yes, a thing," she said "It's a bit long to be called a letter and it doesn't feel right calling it a book." Kate got up from the chair, still clutching the phone to her ear. "Now? Of course, if you want." She sounded surprised. "Or we can do tomorrow morning? It's Saturday tomorrow, the kids can all play together. Jack's not home until tea time." Kate reached for the kettle, cradling the phone between her shoulder and chin as she filled it and turned it on. "Then we'll see you both for lunch? Take care, Lily." Kate pulled the phone from her ear and thumbed the button to disconnect. She made herself a tea and sat drinking it while she thought about what she had just read.

# 4. Control

*On Saturday morning Kate lay awake in bed, watching as the sun rose to shine through the closed curtains. She gazed at the ceiling and sighed at her sleeplessness. Sounds of children starting to stir drifted into the room. She turned her head to see the red numbers on the clock change. Still far too early, and too little sleep.*

*The door creaked open slowly and Hayley crept in. Even at almost eleven years old, she still liked to come for a cuddle in the mornings if she could. Kate shifted over to let her in as they listened to the sounds of the house waking up.*

*Tom couldn't find any socks.*

*Susan wanted to wear a dress.*

*Cameron was hunting for Tom's socks.*

*"Mum!" called out Cam's voice. "We're putting the telly on!" Kate heard him throw something at Tom and she assumed it was socks from the sound they made they bounced off the wall. Kate listened to them thunder down the stairs and, tangled in thoughts and memories, didn't yell at them.*

*Hayley wriggled free and fled from the room, giggling as she called to Susan. The required dress was found and the girls headed downstairs where an argument over the TV channel ensued. Kate sighed and hauled herself from the folds of the warm duvet. She pulled on clothes and made her way downstairs.*

*Her eyes slid past the edge of the card folder peeping out from between the cookery and gardening books, refusing to see it. Kate stuck her head into the living room.*

*"Turn that off." Her voice was firm. "All of you need breakfast." Kate turned and retreated to the kitchen, where increasingly tall, and close-to-adult children were finding bowls, cereal, spoons and milk. She made them all sit at the kitchen table for breakfast.*

*The boys wandered out into the garden and wanted to dig the vegetable bed. Susan and Hayley happily vanished upstairs. After she made sure the boys washed up properly, Kate pulled out the folder to read a bit more before Lily arrived for lunch.*

I woke in the dark. I could hear his breathing as he lay in the bed, his head on the pillows next to me. His weight pulled at the sheets and blankets, distorting the shape of the bed so I rolled into him as soon as I relaxed. I turned over and tried to pull the covers over myself, one side of me was very cold. His arm snaked out and rested its weight on my back. His hand gripped my shoulder and I was pinned. I wriggled onto my back but his arm remained flung over me. He grumbled in his sleep and his grip on my shoulder tightened but he didn't fully wake up. I lay there, awake now and unable to get comfy enough to get back to sleep. I stared at the dark ceiling and listened to the night. Apart from his breathing and shifting in his sleep there were other noises.

I could hear the beating of my own heart in my ears, the hiss of my own breathing. I heard the crackle of the fire in the other room and beyond that, footsteps outside in the corridor. It wasn't that early then if the fortress was awake and moving. I could almost hear voices, but I couldn't hear the words being spoken. As I lay there listening to the sounds of a large household stirring, I felt very alone. The seasons were turning with a painful regularity. I had been with Ametsam for two winters. I wondered what my children were doing, how much time had passed for them? Then he woke and the bubble burst.

"I want to go and see my children," I murmured as he came fully awake.

"What for?" he asked. "Are you not happy here?" He hauled himself up to sitting in the bed, leaning on the wall behind us. He looked sideways at me, expecting an answer.

"Of course I'm happy here with you." I meant it, I was happy. I loved him; I had everything I could ever want. But I missed my kids. "I only want to visit them. I'll come straight back. I could bring them here." He even seemed to consider it for a moment.

"No," he said and I thought I heard regret in his voice. I was certain I saw regret in his face. "They would distract you. They would deflect attention from us. They would confuse the line of succession." I must have allowed my confusion to show on my face more clearly than I thought. "If your existing children come here before we have an acknowledged heir then it will look like I am acknowledging them as mine as well. It will look like I make them my own. I can't risk that. Any heir that is apparent here must be of my bloodline. It is vital that power here remains with those who carry the bloodline magic. You do understand that don't you?" I nodded, swayed by his words. I still wanted to see them, and you.

I very much wanted to see you again, to hug you close. I wanted to sit in your kitchen drinking sweet tea and eating cheap biscuits. I wanted to wait outside the school for my kids and lean on the railings, chattering about nothing. I wanted to lumber Jack with all four children and drag you out to the pub and get very, very drunk.

I said nothing of those feelings to him then. "I do understand. I truly do," is what I said to him.

"Don't forget that time passes differently here," he went on, placating me, soothing my feelings. "You can live a lifetime here and return within days of when you left. You can go back so they won't have even missed you. I promise you, Sam. Only a few short days will have passed at most in your world." He took my hand in one of his and with his other he cradled my face so I couldn't look away from him. "We have all the time you could ever want together." He lowered his face to mine and I was lost in his kiss.

We didn't make it to breakfast that morning and by lunchtime I had forgotten any idea of seeing my children. All my homesickness was wiped away by his attentions. I had not believed the human body to be capable of such heights of passion but that morning he surpassed my wildest imaginings.

"Ah, my Maiden of the Flowers," he sighed as we lay there. I was exhausted but exhilarated. I lay cradled in his arm, curled against his side, an arm draped across his chest. "Perhaps this time my seed will be sown," he rumbled over the top of my head.

"Mmmm I hope so." I snuggled closer to him. I sincerely meant it. I would have been overjoyed at that moment if I had conceived. But I hadn't and a couple of weeks later it was obvious, again.

During the time that I bled he avoided me and I was like a prisoner in my rooms. It happened every month. He didn't even try to hide his disgust that I would allow my body to release his seed like that, that I would deny him his right to a legitimate heir.

"You do this on purpose!" he raged at me that time.

"It is just the human way." I tried to explain to him. "Each month my body prepares as if for a child and then if none is created then I shed the preparation no longer needed."

"You reject my seed!" He took that as a personal rejection. "You do not even want to bear my child. You deny me." He paced as he raged at me and I tried not to flinch. He had not hit me and I had no reason to believe he ever would but his anger was turbulent and unstable.

"Ametsam, you're frightening me." I pleaded with him. The look he flung at me was hurt and barbed with pain. "I do not deny you on purpose. You must understand that?" I reached out for him but he pulled away. He folded his arms tightly across his chest and stood glowering into the fire. His mouth was pressed into a flat, thin line and he quivered with barely suppressed tension.

"I understand nothing that you say woman!" he spat. "I see that your body discards my seed as it sheds your blood." And he stalked from my rooms. I didn't see him for several days after that. I felt rejected. I stewed and went over my words to him. Had I said the wrong thing? Deep down I knew there was nothing I could do or say to make it better but I still sat in my rooms and over analysed it. I replayed the whole thing over and over in my head.

I tried to go out for a walk to clear my head but was stopped before I reached the main doors.

"I'm sorry Respected Consort." The warrior standing there apologised. "I am instructed to make sure you remain within the walls." He stepped firmly between me and the outside, his hand lightly resting on a sword hilt. His intent was plain. My heart thundered hard against my ribs. The blood drained from my face and my guts clenched round the sudden ball of ice that formed there. My hands shook and my legs wobbled alarmingly. I took a series of deep, calming breaths.

"Is there a problem Warrior?" I asked him, naming him according to his role as was the way of the folk in the fortress. "By whose orders am I to remain within the fortress?" He had the courtesy to look uncomfortable. He did not shuffle, nor remove his hand from his sword; but his eyes slid away from my direct gaze and heat flushed his face.

"It is the Masters orders, my lady." He wouldn't meet my look directly. "You are to remain within the fortress unless he gives new orders. I am to restrain you if needed." Finally his eyes met mine and there was a plea in them. "Please don't let that happen. I don't want to have to do that."

I nodded to him. "I won't put you in that position, my Warrior." I said quietly. It wasn't his fault. He was just doing as he was told. "I will return to my rooms and I will discuss the matter with Ametsam when he returns to me." I turned on my heel and strode away on shaky legs. To hide the trembling I stomped along the corridor as if I felt more anger than fear. I flung open the door and then slammed it shut behind me. I had pulled on a long cloak as I prepared for my stroll and I pulled it off now and carelessly threw it at a chair. It pooled there in a heap of crumpled fabric.

I stood and stared at the fire. My mind was whirling with possibilities, whirling so fast I couldn't hold onto a single thought long enough to explore it properly. I sat in the cloak-free chair. I got up again. I poked the fire. I added a log. I poked it again. I paced the room. My fear was growing into panic. I had made him truly angry this time. The panic ate at me until it consumed me and I could no longer think past his anticipated anger.

There was food on the table; it must have arrived while I was talking at the doors. I sat and spread rich yellow butter on a thick slice of warm bread. I added a large chunk of tasty cheese and ate it distractedly as I tried to settle my madly spinning brain. I left the wine unopened and drank clean, clear water instead. Eventually the day passed into evening and Ametsam still didn't come to my rooms. No-one came to my rooms. So I paced and stewed. I poked my head out of the doors a couple of times to see warriors wandering up or down the corridor. They looked more like guards. None of them acknowledged me but they looked up as my door opened. There was no friendship or respect in their eyes. I wondered what he'd said to them about me. I knew they'd never tell me, but I burned to know. I let myself explore what might happen if I tried to go out again in the morning. There was no point going now, it was dark and probably cold.

He left me restricted to my rooms for almost a week. There was a guard on my door who told me daily it was for my own safety. I didn't believe a word he said, although I did believe that Ametsam was capable of doing me harm while he was gripped by the rage I had seen as he paced before my fire. I pleaded deadly boredom and begged some spun and dyed wool and needles from the guard.

I began to knit myself a serape. I felt a bit lost without a proper pattern but I'd managed the sweater before, I could do it. The wool was lanolin rich and the skin on my hands soaked it up as I worked. The wool was fabulous to work with, rich in both texture and colour. I established a repeating geometric pattern in my knitting and let my hands work while my mind stilled. I found knitting meditative. The needles clicked together in a regular uninterrupted rhythm as they always did, almost moving of their own accord. The wool flowed through my fingers, easing from the balls I had wound. The skeins of wool still lay draped over the backs of my other chair. Ametsam wouldn't like that. He'd say it made my rooms look like those of a serving woman. I played with that idea for a while before I realised that I didn't care. Ametsam hadn't been in these rooms for days, neither had anyone else that I cared to invite to linger longer than it took them to deliver food, drink, or clear away.

I was absorbed in my knitting when the door creaked open again. I ignored it as I had been ignoring it for the past few days. Whoever it was would leave whatever they had brought, that I hadn't asked for, and then they would leave. The pattern had become monotonous in its regularity. A boy bearing a load of wood edged past me and carefully placed it in the basket by the side of the fire. His eyes flicked to meet mine and he ventured a smile. I returned it warmly and his tentative smile broke into a grin before he fled. He had a tooth missing and it made for a child's gappy smile that warmed my heart. I thanked him as I hadn't bothered thanking anyone else and his face lit up. A few words from a relative stranger made such a difference to this child's day. I wondered briefly who he was, where he lived and what other jobs he did around the place. I'd not seen him before but the people in the fortress changed all the time.

I slept alone for those nights. I was refused exit from my rooms. I insisted I needed fresh air and was told they would bring my request to the Master's attention. I craved company and yet I relished my solitude. I hoped he would relent and return to me, that he hadn't found another consort. I tied myself in knots with every day that passed when I didn't see him.

Then one day I awoke as the light flared at the end of my bed. The Portal opened silently but the sudden flare of brilliant light had stabbed through my closed eyelids to awaken me. I startled and sat bolt upright, clutching at the quilted bedspread. He stepped from the light and stood at the foot of my bed with a grin stretching across his face.

"Ametsam?" I whispered.

"Dress yourself," he commanded. "Wear the purple dress with the long sleeves, it makes your eyes flash." He stood and watched while I did so. All the time the Portal stood open, flickering and iridescent at the edge of my vision. It hurt to look directly at it, like staring at the sun. I pulled the long, elegant purple dress on and slipped soft shoes onto my feet. As I straightened he held out a hand with the palm uppermost.

"Take my hand," he purred. It wasn't a suggestion. He beckoned me and I went to him. I placed my hand in his and his clawed fingers closed around mine in a firm grip. His other hand came round to caress my cheek and I shivered at his touch.

"I've missed you," I tried to tell him but he cut off my words with a finger placed on my lips.

"I wish to show you something," he said as he pulled me towards the Portal. I followed him. I had no choice. His hold on my hand was like an iron vice but padded with velvet. I stepped into the second Portal I had ever used. It would not be the last.

The air thickened, making it harder to breathe, just like before. The disorientation was the same. I had no idea where I was and if he had let go I felt I would just float off and be lost for ever. The idea was tempting. I considered whether these Portals could be formed to go anywhere or whether they had to have fixed points of origin and destination. Were they focused on a physical item like the oak tree, or a distinct location like the glade? I had only ever seen Ametsam form one of these Portals so I believed that only he could do it. Unless I could find the mysterious and dangerous Mistress Lilith, he was my only way home. If I still wanted to go home? I wasn't sure.

We walked in the light for a few steps and then the other side began to show through the bright white light. I heard rushing water. I smelled green grass. I saw the open sky. I clung to him and was giddy with excitement. We strode from the opening Portal onto soft green grass. The wide expanse was ringed with trees. This was a wooded world after all. There was a freshness and dampness to the air and the rushing water was louder as I placed my foot onto the grass. He relaxed his grip on my hand as he waved the Portal closed behind us with a nonchalant flick of his wrist. He didn't even look at it. I didn't pull my hand free of his but let my palm lie gently against his. He tugged his hand free first and took my shoulders to turn me around. The sight I beheld there was breathtaking.

We stood in a glade. We had stepped onto grass surrounded by trees. Behind us was a gush of water which grew from the earth like magic. It bubbled from the top of the rocks and cascaded down amongst the trees which clung to the sparse soil beside the flow of water. Constantly sprayed and damp they were a luxuriant green but, with the soil continually washed away from their roots, they were short and stocky.

The bubbling of the water captivated me. It flowed from the rock in a sparkling rush. I could smell the freshening of the air that it created. The bright spring sunlight glinted on each droplet of water as it escaped. I gasped at the sheer beauty of it and I felt his hands squeeze my shoulders gently.

"I knew you would love it." His voice breathed softly as his lips moved down to delicately graze my neck. I felt the involuntary shivery tingle run down my spine from that not-unexpected touch. He stroked that sensitive spot at the base of my neck with a single, careful clawed finger. A hand snaked round my waist to lay flat on my stomach and I felt the muscles there twitch under his palm. I was held firmly against him, his chest pressed up to my back. I could feel him breathing, I could feel his heart beating. His mouth on my skin left heat that quickly cooled and chilled. I tried to pull away, intending to turn and return his attentions. But he pressed closer, murmuring, "You don't want to go anywhere my little flower. You will stay right here."

As his voice purred in my ear, I felt like icy water had been dashed in my face. This was the man who had ranted at me, who had confined me to my rooms. What was I doing?

"Actually, I do." I spoke more firmly than I felt. "Please let me go." His hand on my stomach explored the fabric of my dress. "Ametsam, I don't want this. Please stop that. We need to talk."

"Talking can wait," he rumbled and he carried on.

"I said no!" I insisted.

"I said talking can wait," he insisted in return, his hands continuing to explore. I pulled free from him only to have him strike like a snake and grab my wrist as I twisted away. "I am Master here and I will have my seed grow in you. I will have an heir and you will bear him."

I tugged at my wrist without any success. His hand was locked tightly around it. He didn't grip any tighter or pull back but he held me there implacably until I gave up. As I stopped pulling at him he smiled, but there was a cruelty there I hadn't seen before. He eased his arm towards his chest so I was forced to come closer to him. I felt my legs shake and my stomach turn to ice. He reached out his other hand and a clawed finger pricked at the soft underside of my jaw, tilting my head up to his smiling face. With a flick of his wrist he twisted my arm painfully behind me and pinned me to his solid chest. His claw teased round to the back of my neck, where he stroked that sensitive place again. This time there was a distinct tingle and I wonder if he used a magic then. Looking back now, I am certain of it. A warmth spread through me, creating a shiver of anticipation. The hand on my neck slid fingers round to cradle the back of my head as I felt my rising panic evaporate into nothing; less than a memory.

I saw my own hand come up to caress his cheek and he half turned to kiss my palm without taking his eyes from mine. At some point he had released my wrist and waved a gesture behind me. A rough, but large, tent appeared and he pushed us towards it. I went willingly then, I wouldn't have gone willingly a few moments before. I moved like I was in a dream and he got what he wanted.

The talking waited.

I came back into focus lying on my back staring up at blank canvas. It moved in the wind and the light behind it was dappled. He was not there but I heard someone moving outside. I turned my head sideways and saw a shape silhouetted against the wall of the tent. It was him. He was just the other side of the canvas. I turned over and went back to sleep. I could still hear the waterfall cascading its torrent close by. I dozed for what seemed like hours until the sun felt like it was directly overhead. Hot and sticky I grudgingly got out of the pile of blankets he had conjured up and went to pull the dress back on. The flap at the front of the tent opened and Ametsam thrust his head in through the gap.

"You're awake," he commented, stating the obvious. I grunted at him. He stepped fully into the tent and I saw he was still naked. "Come," he commanded and he reached down and heaved me to my feet. I was led by the hand, naked, across the grass. I looked around me in horror, fully expecting there to be warriors watching.

He never went anywhere without a few of his warriors as escort. I saw nothing but trees. "There's no-one there, we are alone." He meant to reassure me but I still felt very exposed. The grass was damp and cool on the soles of my feet. I couldn't remember the last time I had gone barefoot anywhere. Even in my own home I tended to wear slippers or shoes as a protection from the perpetual lethal Lego littering the floor. I longed to simply stand and wriggle my toes in the short green leaves but he towed me along inexorably. His pace was just faster than I was comfortable with and I stumbled every few steps.

He stopped without warning at the edge of the pool and caught me as I almost fell. He scooped me up and threw me into the water. I plunged down under the cold water, the breath driven from my lungs by the force of water and the icy shock. I felt my bare feet touch the slime at the bottom. My eyes were open and I saw the bubbles rise from my gasping mouth. The awareness that I had never learned to swim was oozing slowly into my brain as I watched the bubbles and the gently sweeping water weed. I had an idea that I needed to follow the bubbles, that up would be a good direction to travel in.

Something clutched at my trailing ankle and I startled, taking water into my lungs as I did. I tried to look down but my head couldn't work out which way was down. I flailed madly to free my leg and I felt the grip move up my leg. Then I really panicked. Something had hold of me in there. My eyes were still open and desperately trying to see what had me. Arms wrapped round my waist and I was turned round. I had a glimpse of a green face and then a mouth was firmly sealed to mine. Sweet life-giving air was smoothly breathed into my lungs. Then she released me and gave a gentle push so I drifted to the surface. I could see the sunlight drifting closer and my chest felt like it could burst. Yet I couldn't work out how to move my arms or legs to get closer to the air. I began to drift down again and I paddled madly but only succeeded in becoming disorientated. Then that green face was near me again. She took my face in her cool hands and breathed for me once again before towing me near to the surface. A gentle push and the surface was there.

My head broke the tension at the barrier between water and air and I came up gasping the rich, damp air into my straining lungs. I sank once more and felt her push me up again before Ametsam waded into the water to haul me out. I stumbled from the water and fell against him, spluttering. I doubled over and coughed the water from my lungs, vomiting it forth as I expelled that which should not be in there. He held me as I decided air was better to breathe than water. Then he sat me shaking on the grass as he fetched a blanket.

"I thought all humans could swim?" he asked as he draped the warm wool round my shoulders. I managed to shake my head as I struggled to get my breath back through a raw throat. "Lilith loved the water," he mused.

"Well, I don't." I coughed and spat out another mouthful of what tasted like water weed. It hit the grass beside me with a wet splat and I felt the shivering begin. "I'm too cold," I stammered through chattering teeth. He waved the tent into nothing and a Portal opened nearby. He scooped me up, still wrapped in the blanket, and stepped into the Portal. I leaned my head on his shoulder, I couldn't hold on as my arms were pinned in the blanket. He took us back into my bedroom and he lay me down there, shivering uncontrollably now, on the bed and heaped blankets and my quilted bedspread over me. I heard him shouting through the open door but the words made no sense to my buzzing ears. I tried to burrow further into the bed but strong hands hauled me back onto my pillows again. After a time I slept. My dreams were bright and too-sharp.

There followed a period of half-waking dream like snatches of memory for me. I think the chill and shock of the sudden submersion in the icy water had made me sick for a time. My body, overcompensating for the cold, had developed a fever and it took a few days to break.

One day I felt well enough to get up from my sick bed and I staggered to sit in one of the chairs by the fire. There was no sign of Ametsam and I don't recall him having been there while I was sick. At the noise of my movement the door opened a fraction and a face peered in at me. Then the door closed again and the face was gone. Within what felt like seconds, a tap came at the door and it was eased open. The boy who had brought the wood that time peeked in before venturing a foot across my threshold. He bore a tray with a covered bowl, a plate of soft bread and a steaming mug. The mug was filled with rich beef broth, the bowl with sweet porridge. I motioned for him to put the tray on the table and he drew the other chair over so I could sit comfortably. I thanked him and he scuttled from the room as if scalded, but his smile made me smile in return. I carefully spooned the smooth porridge to my lips and savoured every mouthful until my stomach complained just before I finished the bowl. I took the bread and broth back to the fire and sat there cradling them. I dipped the bread in the mug and ate it slowly. After draining the last of the rich, salty broth from the mug I was weary and shivered again. So I made my way back to my bed. But I had been up, I had eaten. I would recover. It would take time but I would recover.

After that my life took on a new pattern. Each morning I woke to find breakfast laid out on the table in front of my fire. My mornings were my own but if I ventured from my rooms I was escorted. The escort was always courteous and always lightly armed. This was for my own safety of course. I understood that. After all, they told me I had come too close to death after the fall into the pool.

*Kate shivered and laid down the pages.*

*Sam had come close to not returning at all. As the realisation hit home, Kate sank her head onto her hands and cradled it. She sat there with her eyes closed and let her mind drift, unwilling to contemplate the inevitability of the whole thing.*

"I know how this ends," she muttered to herself "Why am I reading it?"

"Because otherwise you'll never know what happened."

"I know." Kate replied to Sam's memory echoing inside her head.

Kate was bending over the oven, checking on baking potatoes, when the back door burst open and Tom leaned in.

"Andrew's here!" he yelled. "He's with us."

"I know." She smiled past him as she straightened up, towards Lily, framed in the doorway, behind Tom.

Lily grinned. "Smells like potatoes?" she guessed, standing aside as Tom raced past her and out through the still-open kitchen door. The two women hugged a greeting.

"Been reading more?" Lily nodded to the papers in a neat pile on the table.

"Yes." Kate nodded. "It's hard work though and I'm really not sure why I am." Lily squeezed her friends shoulder before moving away to busy herself with the kettle.

"Because otherwise we'll never know what happened." Lily's words echoed the exact words Kate had thought just a short while before and Kate shook her head, laughing at the wash of déjà vu.

# 5. Rebellion

    *Lily had a way of just taking over that sometimes irritated, but today Kate enjoyed the familiarity as she placed the document back into the slim card folder. She started to rise from the chair but Lily's hand came over her shoulder to take the folder, replacing it with a mug of tea which Kate hadn't noticed being made.*

    *"Stay there, enjoy the tea." Lily slipped the folder into a space between the cookery books wandered over to the door to yell at the boys to come in and get washed. Then all was chaos and turbulence as the mayhem of feeding five children and two adults*

*commenced. It wasn't until later, when Lily sat Kate down on the green sofa with a mug of hot sweet tea and handed her the folder again, that Kate managed to read more.*

I took several days to begin to recover but then developed a wet cough which left me shaking and dizzy. There were iron bands round my chest. Or rather, it felt like that. It was such hard work to drag air in that there were times I almost gave up and didn't bother. But the healers came and beat my back until the phlegm came up. They forced me to drink bitter teas and suffer regular steaming. They burned herbs in my rooms until I couldn't bear the stench in my nostrils. Some made me sneeze uncontrollably. Through that recovery time I barely saw Ametsam. His visits were brief and he mainly talked with whoever was forcing me to drink whatever concoction they had decided might work that day. I was miserable. I thought of you more often.

At some point, although my chest was still painful, my fever finally subsided and stayed away. I heard the healers coldly declare that I would probably live now, that the worst was over. Ametsam was there. The healer turned from him and looked me up and down with an appraising eye.

"You have lost too much weight through this," she announced and I winced. "You must rebuild the muscle on your bones and then add a fat layer. I will see that the kitchens are instructed accordingly." With that she stalked out. Ametsam shrugged in a half apology and followed her out, closing the door behind him. I heard his voice rumble indistinctly. His words were muffled and I thought I heard a second voice reply. But I was tired and I let my head fall onto my chest where I sat in the chair by the fire. I must have slept soundly. When I eased open my gummy eyes I found the fire built up, the wood basket full and a blanket tucked round me. There was warm mulled wine sitting in a jug by the fire. The steam wafted towards me and I breathed it in with a smile. A covered plate revealed sweet pastries also keeping warm by the fire.

I helped myself to a mug of the wine and one of the pastries. The filling was sweet fruit and honey. It burst onto my tongue as I bit down, coming close to dripping down my chin. The flaking pastry melted on my tongue. It was delicious. After I'd eaten, I took my blanket back to bed. I slept again. I slept a lot for several days, rising only to eat, drink and use the toilet really. But I slowly felt more human and less sick. I begged needles and assorted thread and I sat by my fire and mended the small tears in some of my clothing. I patched the knee of my favourite trousers. I took up the dress that had always been just a tiny bit long. I dug out my knitting and I finished my warm serape. I fringed it and often sat with it draped around my shoulders as I kept busy.

I went for short walks into the meadow but there was always a warrior at my elbow. Still, I couldn't walk fast or far so the company was warranted I suppose. It felt more like a guard than a nursemaid though and I rankled at it. I put my irritability down to my illness and simply glowered at them. I put every bit of venom I could muster into sideways glances at my guards on those walks. But either they didn't notice or there wasn't that much venom. Either way it had no effect. Every time I left my rooms I acquired a silent shadow within a few steps.

The first few times it happened I expected and even welcomed it. It made sense to me to have an escort. I was recovering slowly from an illness that left my legs wobbly. Ametsam was worried. He must be. He hadn't been to see me often, but he was busy. It was understandable. I warped my thoughts to accommodate this thinking. I made the reality I wanted to see.

None of my guards wished to talk or explain things to me. Time after time I was told, "You must discuss that with the Master." Oh they were always courteous. They always offered me the respect due to the Respected Consort of their beloved Master. But the sweet side of life began to sour as I felt more trapped. Frustrated at my slow journey back to full health and at the constrictions placed on my movements, my thoughts drifted more and more to my old life and my other family. I found it difficult to accept that time would pass differently here and that only a few days had passed for you and my children. I longed to see you, to be sure that no time had passed for you, to know that you weren't grieving for me.

Ametsam finally came back to me some weeks later. He just turned up one day, bearing a woven basket full of food and a bottle of wine. He stood in my doorway and looked down on me as I sat knitting.

"Why is my consort reduced to that?" he demanded. "My consort should lack for nothing. Why are you insisting on mending? Why do you ask to perform such menial tasks?" He stepped into the room but I didn't put down my knitting. I had almost finished the row when he swatted the needles from my hands. I pulled back smarting fingers where his hand had caught mine. He balled my knitting in his fists and threw it onto the fire.

"Ametsam!" I cried "What did you do that for?" I screwed up my nose against the acrid stench now coming from the smouldering wool on the fire. There was no rescuing it now. He had hurled it into the centre of a roaring blaze. Thick smoke was curling from it and was more than the chimney could cope with so the room was filling with choking, bitter smoke. My eyes streamed with tears and my vision was blurred by the think pungent cloud. I felt the irritation in my still sensitive lungs and the spasm of the cough began. I expelled the smoke and all my air in a spluttering fit. I gasped in more smoke in a reflex and choked again. I heard him speak but my ears were filled with my panicking heartbeat and I couldn't understand him. The sound of someone retching was close by and eventually I realised I was hearing myself. I heard the wheezing as I struggled to cough and drag air into me. My ears buzzed and what little I could see through my tearing eyes was starting to darken. I felt his hand on my neck, felt the claws scrape across my skin. He tugged at the back of my dress and I couldn't work out what he was trying to do until my knees and then my feet left the floor. A tightness binding my ribs should have told me that he had hold of the back of my dress but by then I was close to passing out. He must have hauled me by the scruff of the neck right along the corridor and out through the double doors.

My eyes slowly cleared to see the sky looming blue above me. I dragged clean air into my straining lungs and tried not to cough. It felt like my throat was pinched closed. I heaved myself over on to my side and let the cough spasm through me until I retched again. At last it subsided and I was able to properly fill my lungs again. My head pounded and I knew my legs were shaking.

Ametsam stood at the doors looking down at me. He was shaking his head. "Frail human," I thought I heard him mutter, but my ears still buzzed and my heart thumped behind the buzz. I stared up at him blearily. He was still holding the basket. I uncurled myself and sat up. My head spun but cleared fast enough. I wasn't going to risk standing yet though. The rapid beating of my heart in my ears steadied to normal and after a few more short coughing fits I could breathe without gasping. He pushed the basket into the hands of a watching warrior and told her to get me back to my rooms when the smoke had cleared. I watched him walk away. I was a little dazed but I could see he didn't really care once he was sure I wasn't going to die.

As soon as he was out of sight the warrior brought me fresh water and made certain I was recovered before sending someone to check my rooms. She stayed with me and seemed to care. I used more of the water to wipe my face and wash the smoky grit from my eyes.

"Shall I arrange for bathing water for you?" the warrior asked. "Lavender is excellent oil for soothing burns and irritation," she suggested. "My grandmother used it often and I think saved my brother from serious scarring after he slipped and put his hand in the fire at home. It was his sword hand."

"A bath would be wonderful." I smiled up at her and held out a hand to be helped to my feet. She willingly obliged. "Lavender is used in my home too. I love the scent. Thank you." Standing was a little too high up and my head spun again. She took my arm and supported me more than I felt I needed but less than I wanted.

Together we stumbled back to my rooms. They had been declared clear of smoke but the pungent stink was still prevalent in the air. "I will send in some scented candles to help remove the smell," she promised and then she left me alone once again. Whatever Ametsam had planned was clearly not going to happen. She had left the basket on the table. On investigation it looked like a sumptuous picnic hamper for two. I pulled some of the food out and ate it. I left the wine corked and drank water instead. It was easier on my raw throat. As I ate and drank my bath arrived, followed by a stream of people with steaming buckets. I made sure I thanked them all for their prompt delivery but there was no reaction.

I lay in the scented hot water and let the steam ease my chest. From behind the screens I heard someone enter and walk through my room. It unnerved me until I heard her voice.

"It's only me Respected Consort." It was the woman warrior from earlier. "I am just lighting the candles for you." I called back to acknowledge her and thank her. Then I lay back and enjoyed my bath as the scent from the candles eased through the lavender from the bath.

It wasn't long before I was back on my feet and being escorted out walking again. Defiantly I asked for more wool and needles and began to knit again. This time I was more careful and I kept a small wooden chest by the fire. I took up the more ladylike pursuit of pointless needlepoint. The tapestry sat at the top of the chest but there was ample room to hide the knitting underneath, at the bottom of the chest. That project grew slowly. I worked on it only when he wasn't likely to be around. When I thought I had a good stretch of time to myself I knitted. I had plenty of time for thinking and with being left alone I think I started to shake off his magical influence. For the first time since he appeared at my car window my head was beginning to feel clear.

I had simply accepted so much, taken him at his word. He had controlled my life, dictated what and when I ate, where I slept and who with. How much of that was his use of the magic fogging my mind and how much was my simple gullibility, I am not sure. I would like to blame him for it but I suspect that at least part of the blame was mine to bear. Each time he was absent for a few days my thoughts would clear as if a veil was lifted. I would plan what to say to him, I would sit and knit as I rehearsed it all in my mind. I was going to ask him to let me visit home, I would come back to him, I would promise. He was going to see the truth in my eloquent words and he would open a Portal and I would walk through.

Then he would appear at my door with a meal and the planning and rehearsal vanished like smoke and I said nothing. It was as if he waved away my mind as he came close. I did everything I could to please him but it was never enough. Whatever I did, it was never enough.

There came a day when I was so distracted with my thoughts turning to you and the children that he asked me, "What is wrong with you today? You are so distracted I may as well not be here." Always he phrased things as if it was my entire fault. When I took a moment to collect my thoughts and to think of what to say, he berated me. "Are you sick again? Tell me, what is the problem? Do I not please you?" He stood with his fists resting on his hips. His scowl softened and he relaxed enough to sit in the chair. I took the chance that had just presented itself.

"Ametsam," I began. "I need to see my children. They must miss me and I miss them. I'm homesick." I didn't mention you, Kate, or anyone else, just my children. "I just want to see them. You could come too. We could bring them back here." I tried to sound reasonable but his face darkened in anger before I had finished speaking.

His nostrils flared as he sucked in a breath. "I have told you why your children cannot come here. It will confuse the order of succession until you have borne my heir, which is still noticeable in its absence. I see no swelling of your belly. Every month my seed is rejected. Every month my warriors laugh at my impotence. I will not have it."

"I must see them," I insisted. "They are my children, my blood. I simply must see them Ametsam or I'll go mad. I have to see them. I have to know they're OK. I have to be sure that it has been only days for them."

"You accuse me of deceit?" he growled angrily "You believe I would purposefully deceive you? I told you that only days will have passed for them. You think I would lie to you?" He was still sitting but his hands clenched back into fists and I was aware of his strength. I remembered all too well how he had apparently effortlessly hauled me from that room using only one hand. The muscles in his arms, across his shoulders and chest were swollen and tense. The veins in his neck stood up. His jaw was thrust forwards, accentuating the scaling on his face, as the flickering light from the fire caught their patterning. His lips pressed together into a thin, raging, bloodless line.

"I don't accuse you of anything," I said, desperate to calm his wrath. "I simply find it difficult to understand how I can have been here these years and only days have passed in my world."

He cut me off with a wave of his hand. "This is your world now. You are my Consort. Not that you are any Lilith, but you are still my Consort and I am Master of this Realm. You will forget any pathetic notion of returning to that other world until after you have produced me an heir." He was on his feet in a single fluid motion and that was the moment when he first struck me.

The back of his hand flew out and impacted on my cheek with sufficient force to knock me and my chair over. I lay there stunned, legs tangled in the chair and the fabric of the dress I had thought he would appreciate. My cheek stung. I lifted a hand to tentatively touch it, expecting to find split flesh and blood there. It felt whole, no leaking blood. I stared up at him as he turned and walked from my room. He slammed the door behind him. I lay there for a long while, unwilling to move. My mind reeled with what he had just done.

Slowly I untangled my legs from the chair frame and from the twisted fabric of the dress. As I did that I started to feel more bruises from the fall. The side of the chair had broken the impact on the floor by causing a bruise all of its own. My hip would be sore as that developed. I sat on the rug in front of the fire and assessed the physical damage. First there was my cheek, I'd need a mirror to check that but at least the skin hadn't split. It was starting to sting though as my shocked numbness wore off a little. The hurt hip was on the opposite side. My shoulder on that side was smarting too where it had hit the wooden floor. An ankle felt twisted from being caught in the chair legs. I reached out my pain-free arm and straightened the chair. Then I tried to get to my feet. Sure enough the ankle threatened to give way and I couldn't put my full weight on it yet.

The assessment of the physical damage was automatic. I knew I distracted myself from thinking about what had actually happened then. My mind stayed on the practical and refused to think about the implications. I could feel my ankle seizing up and my face swelling. I decided that cold water and a cloth would deal with both and went to my door to see if I could get some. I'd ask for it if there was someone there, it would save me trying to limp on a twisted ankle.

The door was locked. I reached it, grabbed the handle and pulled. I almost pulled my arm out of its socket. The door was heavy but had always swung open easily. It never stuck. But I still checked it, more than once. I was reeling from the blow, the fall and now the realisation that I was locked in my rooms.

I hammered on the unyielding wood of the door. I yelled as loudly as I could. The result was that now my hands were sore too and my throat was raw. No-one answered. I could hear voices along the corridor, there were people out there. They ignored me. I wondered what Ametsam had said. I wondered what he had told them. I wondered what they all thought of me now. Eventually, tired and sore I gave up and limped back to my chairs by the fire. I sat in one and put my ankle up on the other. I had some wash water left so I dipped a bit of cloth in that and used it to ease the swelling in my cheek and then my ankle. I should have used an ice pack really but it was better than nothing. The ankle wasn't swelling yet despite my having stumbled about on it. My hands were sore after hitting the door but they were easing. My hip was going to be stiff and bruised. My cheek was swelling. I could see the lump developing beneath my eye.

Several hours later there came a knock at the door. I called out for whoever it was to let themselves in rather than trying to get up. The door opened and the boy came in with a tray of food for me. I watched his eyes widen at the bruise now showing on my face.

"It's fine," I reassured him "Don't worry. It'll heal." This wasn't something a child needed to be concerned with. He nodded but I could see he was unsure. He set down the tray and reluctantly left me alone again. As he moved through the door way I heard the jangle of keys from outside. The door was firmly shut and locked again behind him.

Despondently I inspected the tray. The food was what I normally expected but only enough for me. I would clearly be eating alone. I wasn't surprised. In fact I was relieved. I didn't want to face him just yet and I had become used to eating alone at times. So I sat at my table and I ate. As I chewed I discovered another bruise. His fingers must have caught the edge of my jaw. The bone there felt thick and painful. I hadn't felt that battered since we were at school.

Do you remember that fight I got in? You stood and watched. You didn't wade in, you stood and watched. Then when it was over, when my nose was bleeding and my lip split you were there. You helped me wipe my face and got a soaking wet, but icy cold, cloth to press on it all. That was the last time I had felt that battered.

So I knew that the following day I would be stiff and sore. I would feel worse before I felt better. I ate everything that had been brought. I used the first of the wine to bathe my bruises in case there was a graze. My cheek stung so I thought there may be. I hadn't had the courage to go and look in my bedroom mirror. I didn't want to know what I looked like just then. I knew it would look worse tomorrow. So I dealt with it all as best I could and just hoped. It was all I could do under the circumstances.

I was right. The next day I could barely move when I woke up. Everything ached. I did take a long look in my mirror. The bruise was a lovely rich purple and the flesh on my cheekbone was swollen and puffy. The eye was bloodshot and itchy. My hip and shoulder on the other side were sore but not swollen. The bruising there wasn't as bad. My neck was stiff. I supposed that was from a sort of whiplash effect.

I felt very detached from the whole thing. It was as if I was dreaming and I would wake up at any moment. I ran my tongue around the inside of my mouth. There was a rough spot inside my cheek to match the bruise. But everything else seemed to be where it should be and not harmed. My mouth was dry but I suspected I had slept with it open, the swelling on my cheek making it uncomfortable. He had dealt me a single thoughtless blow and I looked and felt like I'd been in a boxing ring.

But, I told myself, I had made him angry. I had asked to see my children before and he had explained. He'd told me why I couldn't and why they couldn't come to me yet. Stupidly I had asked him again. I had pushed him to change his mind. I stood and stretched to try to ease the stiffness. My shoulder and neck made it difficult to raise my arm over my head so I pulled on soft legging type trousers and a loose tunic. I stuffed my feet into woollen socks purely because they were cold and then added a warm jerkin over the tunic. Ametsam wouldn't approve, it wouldn't feminine enough for him but then I doubted he'd be coming to see me that day. Or maybe he'd come to gloat. Either way I was in too much aching pain to care. I simply wanted to be warm and to not struggle to get undressed again that evening.

I limped out to the other room. The fire had been left to burn low and there was no breakfast there yet. Maybe it was earlier than I thought. I poked at the fire myself and added more wood. The basket was full and would last a few days. I went to try the door again. It was still locked.

Set into the ceiling of my room was a large crystal. It was polished and clear as glass. In fact it may have been glass but Ametsam had told me it was a crystal. It was the base of a light well, part of a set of shafts that ran through the fortress, bringing sunlight to the deepest rooms. I think the crystal either focused or unfocused the light so my room was light when the sun shone. I had a multitude of candles for the nights and dark evenings of winter. He had offered to light my rooms with his magic many times but I loved candle light.

So, it was light enough for me to examine the door, which meant the sun was up, which in turn meant it was late enough that my breakfast should have been on the table by then. Scowling pulled at my cheek, but it didn't stop me. Brows furrowed in both frown and concentration I took a long look at the door that I had barely noticed before. It was made from thick, dark planks of wood. The long tangs to the hinges stretched across all bar the furthest panel. They were held in place by several large headed nails each. There was the familiar large door handle on the side furthest from the hinges. But there was no keyhole, no lock in the inside. Understanding hit me like a dash of cold water. This was a door that could only be locked from the outside, never from inside the room. This was a door that made my rooms a prison. They had always been a prison and I had never seen it before now. Suddenly the space I had been calling my own seemed so much smaller. An air of constraint filled my rooms. I was shocked by how it dramatically altered my perception of my own spaces.

I could hear voices outside so I tapped on the door. The keys jangled, the lock snicked and the door was eased open. An armed warrior stood there. He was stocky with an olive complexion. His hair was cropped short. He scowled in at me.

"What?" he demanded.

I was a little taken aback by his manner. "I am awake and would appreciate some breakfast," I told him in the politest tones I could muster. I deliberately hadn't phrased it as a request, more like an instruction. But he only grunted and yanked the door shut. I listened to him lock it again. I heard laughter through the door and I wondered if I would get any food at all. I was obviously not going to be allowed out.

My door was locked. There were at least two of his warriors standing guard outside in the corridor. They would at least open the door to see what I wanted if I knocked. That was something. It was a start. Perhaps Ametsam would come and see me in a day or so and we could work this out. I knew I had angered him and felt it to be all my own fault. I couldn't change the fact that I couldn't seem to conceive him a child but I could try harder to appease him. I could keep my thoughts of you and of my children to myself.

I had retreated to my chair and was sitting by the fire when the door opened again. The stocky warrior brought in a bowl with a spoon stuck into it and a jug. He was followed by the boy with a load of fire wood. The bowl and jug were banged down onto the table so the contents slopped over the edges. The boy carried his load to my log basket and over-filled it. He tossed the last log directly on to the fire. It made the fire collapse a bit as it settled deep into the flames. Sap from the log hissed as the heat caught it. These logs weren't the fully dry ones I was used to then. I thanked him and got the usual shy smile.

"Boy!" The stocky warrior's voice was harsh. The boy turned and received a cuff round the ear for daring to speak to me. I drew a breath to defend him but the look I got from the man was enough to silence my voice before I spoke. He grabbed the boy's collar and literally dragged him from the room. I suspected I would never see him again. As the door slammed and the now-familiar jangle of keys was heard, I ventured to investigate the bowl and jug. The jug held clear, fresh water. I had cups in my rooms already. The bowl was at least full and deep. But it was warm porridge, beginning to congeal. I took it over to the fire and put it as near the flames as I dared in an attempt to try and reheat it a little. After a while I gave up and ate it anyway. At least it was easy on my sore mouth.

So my days changed again. My door remained locked and guarded. I was right in my suspicions, I never saw that boy again. I hoped he hadn't been beaten or made to suffer for daring to smile at me. I was given food regularly but it was plain stuff unlike the rich meals I had shared with Ametsam before. But in the time I was left alone in that space I healed. My bruises and aches faded and vanished.

*Lily stood leaning on the door-frame and watched as Kate was lost in the pages. She crept quietly away, ushering children out of the kitchen and into the garden. Susan stood at the back door. Lily watched with a smile as her granddaughter drew a deep breath, gestured with her hands and nodded, apparently satisfied. Then she turned to the stairs and repeated the gesture.*

"Well done." *Lily ruffled Susan's long, blonde hair.*

*The boys stayed outside and weren't too raucous. The girls played quietly in the bedroom. An aura of peace and calm hung about the house and both Kate and Lily basked in it while the others relaxed and let go of recent trauma for a few moments. Kate grinned.*

*"Still need to talk?" Lily asked.*

*"Yes," Kate replied. "But not with kids about."*

*"No problem." Lily stirred sugar into the tea and passed it over. "Monday? After we drop the kids at school?" Kate nodded. "Come over to mine, we can have lunch."*

# 6. Locked up

*He hit her? Kate thought, half stunned by the idea that wasn't that hard to believe. She knew he'd done something. She'd seen the bruises Sam had when she made it back and not all of them had been fresh. Why was it so hard to read about it, to almost feel the blow and the pain? Rolling her shoulders she winced at the ache in them. She felt tired, more than tired, verging on exhausted, but she knew she wouldn't sleep yet.*

*Kate stood in the dark kitchen with her hand on the light switch and her head tipped to one side. She could hear rain pattering gently on the windows. A smile creased her face as she listened.*

*As the rest of the house slept, Kate retrieved Sam's manuscript from its hiding place. As soon as tea was steaming in her mug, she sat at the table to read some more.*

As the last traces of yellow faded from my cheek he came to my door. I was sitting by the fire, finishing off a cushion I'd made to keep myself from being too bored. I didn't stop as he walked in. I sat and carried on sewing but I did look up and smile at him. I had embroidered the cushion with a stylised tree in my favourite autumnal colours. A clean blue background set the tree against the sky and it was framed with a border of twined vines. I was proud of it. It would fit nicely over the pad that sat on the chair behind my back. The cover on that had caught and torn as I had fallen after he hit me. I winced as I thought of it and glanced up again to see what he was doing. He was standing by the table, setting out food he took from a tray held by the armed warrior beside him.

He caught me looking. "Will you eat with me?" he asked and his voice was surprisingly gentle. When the tray was empty he waved the warrior from the room and turned to face me. He was expecting an answer. I laid down my sewing and slowly rose to my feet.

"I will," I answered him simply. I joined him at the table and he served me my meal with his own hands. He broke the loaf of bread in two and offered me the choice of which half to take. It was a ritualistic action and I paused before taking the one nearest to me. I'm sure it signified something to him but I wasn't sure what. He placed a selection of items on my plate. There was tangy cheese, slices of cold meat that might have been chicken, fresh fruits and some salad-type leaves. He poured a delicately flavoured, dry white wine into a pair of crystal goblets and passed one to sit by my plate. The light from the fire made it glow warmly. The images of the flames reflected in the glass and honey coloured liquid and leant it pseudo warmth as they danced there.

I lifted the glass and a delicate waft of elderflowers drifted up to me. There was an aroma which reminded me of those late spring days when life is rich and full. It smelled of sunshine and the promise of summer. I took a careful sip. It was as full and delicious as it smelled. I let that first sip roll along my tongue, savouring that first taste. It was a fresh young wine, probably only last years. I took another appreciative mouthful before starting on any of the food. The bread was warm and full of seeds. It was rough but soft and full of nutty flavour. I slathered the warm bread with rich, yellow butter that slowly melted into the surface. Then I piled the tangy cheese on top and raised it towards my face. The warmth of the bread made the smells coming from the butter and cheese tantalisingly tempting. I paused and breathed it in for a second before biting. It was a glorious combination of soft warm bread, nutty seedy flavour, rich butter and the bite of the cheese sliced through all of those. It was the perfect complement to itself. I made sure I ate well. The food I had been getting was nowhere near this standard. It made a pleasant change and I enjoyed it as best I could with him sitting across from me. Other than asking me to eat with him he hadn't said a word since entering my rooms. I was wary of him, unsure of his mood.

I had almost convinced myself that the blow was in anger, that it was a one off. But sitting with him and looking at his hands and arms I suddenly wasn't sure. I sat and ate with him, drank with him but each time he moved I felt the flicker of a flinch. I watched him and I was certain he was moving in a way to make that happen. He ate in silence as I did. When we had both finished he cleared away the plates and handed them to the guard on the door. He refilled our wine glasses and moved over to the fire, where he sat down obviously waiting for me to join him. I did. I tried to carefully land in the chair so I could push it a bit further from him. I tried to make it look accidental but I didn't want to be too close to him.

I was suspicious. He hadn't been to see how I was healing, how much he'd hurt me. He sat there, so confident, so self-assured, I knew he wasn't feeling any remorse. I sat and drank the wine he handed me and felt the anger build alongside a rising fear. No-one else could open a Portal. No-one else could get me home. I sipped at my wine as I tried to get my surging feelings under control.

"I am glad to see you," I told him.

"I have missed you," He replied and I knew he lied. He reached out to take my hand and the muscles in my arm twitched before I could stop them. He smiled and took my hand anyway. I know it trembled as it lay clasped in his fist. "Would you like to walk with me tomorrow?" he asked.

I nodded. "I would like that," I managed to answer. I would get out of my rooms and see the sun and sky again. I could take the chance to feel the grass beneath my feet. I smiled at him then. "That would be lovely."

"Then you shall join me after your breakfast in the morning." He rose from his chair with my hand still in his. "Sam?" he spoke my name as a question to get my attention. I lifted my face to meet his steely gaze. "Just in case you doubt that I am in complete control here." He tightened his grip on my hand and I felt the heat of his magic flood into my arm. The muscles from my wrist right up to the base of my skull went into agonising spasm. I cried out in shock and pain. The pain suddenly subsided, leaving me gasping. He smirked cruelly and stalked from the room. I sat and cradled my arm against my chest while the tension in my muscles eased slowly. My head was beginning to pound and I knew a nasty headache was on the way. The door swung shut behind him and I heard the keys in the lock. I uncurled my fingers and let my arm drop down into my lap. I did so hesitantly as if it would spark another wave of pain to move it. I took several deep breaths and forced the bunched muscles to relax. I flexed my fingers away from the palm and for a moment I couldn't bear to look at my hand I was so sure there would be some sort of mark, a burn. I forced myself to look but there was nothing there. The skin was as whole and unblemished as when it had held my wine glass. My hands shook. I bowed my head into my shaking hands and waited for my heart to slow back to normal. It took a long while.

I had known of his magic. I knew some of what it could do. I had seen him open a door between worlds, a door from one place to another in this world. I had seen him draw flame from the sun and ignite a bonfire. I had witnessed his flame driven transformation. The sheer scale of the power I had seen was awe inspiring. But this was more subtle. This was secretive. What he had just done implied a finesse and control that was in opposition to the flamboyance I had seen up till then. It frightened me more than ever. I drank what was left of the wine and then went to rest my thumping head on my bed. I think I slept. If I dreamed I don't remember. My arm was fine once I let it relax and the headache faded.

The following morning I was woken by a clattering of dishes in the other room. Breakfast had arrived. After I had eaten he would be here and we would go out walking. I was torn. On the one hand I was eager to be outside again, to feel the wind on my face, the sun on my skin. On the other hand I would be with the man I had come to fear. The realisation that I would never see you again was trickling into my head. I would never see you or my children again. He had control of the only way home and he wasn't going to use it for that. He had shown a side of himself I had been too stupid to see. I was now isolated and alone. I lay there and listened to the sounds of my breakfast die away. I waited until I was sure the door was closed and locked before I ventured out of my bedroom. I had put on a dark green dress. I knew he preferred dresses. I pulled on my sturdiest boots and bound my hair back with a beaded thong. Then I went to see what he had seen fit to send me for my breakfast.

I was pleasantly surprised. The table held warm soft bread, a pot of creamy butter and another of golden honey. There was a steaming pot of fragrant tea and a basket of fresh fruit. I poured myself a mug of the tea. The aroma that rose from the dark liquid was full of sweetness and fruit with an edge of tart herbs. I added a spoon of honey and stirred it thoughtlessly, while my mind wandered. I tore open the small loaf of bread and inhaled the steam that came from it. The soft fluffy bread must have come straight from the oven it was that hot. I left it for a moment to cool a little before I put butter on it. I sipped at the tea and burned my mouth. I sucked in breath after breath to ease the sting of heat and laughed at myself. I never waited for tea to cool properly, I never had. Steam had stopped rising from the torn loaf so I spread butter on it. The rich yellow eased into the open porous surface leaving it looking darkly moist and tasty. I ate the first half just like that, warm and dripping with butter. The second piece I spread thickly with the golden honey that tasted of the meadow. By then the tea had cooled enough to not scald my mouth any more so I could sip at it slowly. The fruit sweetness was delightful and complimented the honey beautifully and the tart edge was a distinct slice through the syrup the honey left in my mouth. I finished the pot, liberally dosed with what was left of the honey.

I was just draining the tea from the last mug when I heard keys in the door. I swallowed hastily, the tea suddenly bitter and dry as ashes. He filled the doorway. He scowled and I leapt to my feet.

"It is cold." He greeted me. "You will need a cloak." I nearly ran to fetch one. I fumbled in my room to find the forest green one he had said he liked. I flung it around my shoulders, pinning it as best I could in my haste. Then I went to join him.

He offered me his arm. I pulled away not wanting my skin to touch his flesh. I was afraid of what that contact might bring after the previous night. His lips twitched in what might have been seen as a smile.

"You fear me." There was no question in his voice but a self-satisfaction I was almost shocked to hear. The look he threw in my direction was one of careless cruelty and I knew then that he would never let me come home. My heart sank. He reached out and took my hand, placed it on his arm and held it there. I shivered but no pain came. He trapped my hand and wrist there and walked from my rooms. I knew a moment of pure panic as I surrendered to his lead. The twist of ice that formed in the pit of my stomach took longer to dispel than the trembling and shortness of breath. I forced a smile onto my face and knew it looked as false as it truly was. I made my feet move and keep pace with him so he did not pull me along and I did not appear unwilling.

He walked me for most of the morning until we reached a river. It was more of a large stream really. Having been kept to my rooms since my accident I was unfit and tired when we arrived at the stream. I pleaded with him to stop to rest and he sneered at me with a condescending look on his face. He clearly wanted to go further and toyed with the idea of walking until I dropped in my tracks. I wanted to run, to go back to the relative safety of my rooms. I wanted to shrink and be swallowed by the earth we walked upon.

The grass by the stream was short and springy. I felt it soft underneath my boots. I was tired and needed to rest for a while. My pace had slowed but he still held on to my hand. It felt like he would never let me go.

"You are no Lilith." He murmured so softly I barely heard him. "Frail human you are no match for me. My Lilith was a goddess. She matched me in both power and ambition. But you?" He stopped and faced me "You are nothing, mortal, decaying as you live. A little pain and you cower. A little pain and you cannot find the strength to defy me? I watched you. I thought you better than this." His words stung. I had heard more of Mistress Lilith from the few warriors and servants who had bothered to talk with me. She was painted as a cruel woman who ruled through her manipulation and control. This was the woman Ametsam claimed as worthy to be by his side and so she seemed to me then.

"You are right." I schooled myself to calm. "I am not her. I am me. I am human and I am mortal. I am also tired and wish to rest please." I tugged my hand free and sat by the stream. The grass was a soft as it looked. The water babbled as it coursed over the stony stream bed. It was deeper than it had looked before and I noticed fish swimming amongst the water weed. I had turned my back on him and that was a mistake. I had defied him and then turned my back on him. So I never saw the blow that knocked me over. I felt it. I felt him connect with the back of my head. I do not know if it was his hand or foot but it was hard. My vision swam and the world blurred as I fell forward towards the water. I flung my arms out to stop the fall and was astonished to feel a hand in mine. I was up to my elbows in cold water and someone was holding my hand. The hand on mine was human shaped but green. I let my eyes follow the arm up to a smiling face. A finger of her other hand was placed on her lips in a plea for silence. She was hidden in the reeds at the streams edge. She released my hand and retreated from sight. I was expecting a second blow but it never came. Instead I heard a shout.

"Master!" A warrior came running through the trees. He was breathless and sped at full stretch. He skidded to his knees at Ametsam's feet. He bowed his head and frantically tried to steady his breathing.

Ametsam scowled at him. "What news makes you dare to disturb me when I am with my Consort?" he growled. I saw the man flinch. With his head bowed and his breathing uneven the man stammered out his message. I couldn't hear or understand the words spoken but the effect on Ametsam was dynamic. "You will stay with her until I return. If I am not here by sundown take her back to the fortress." He flung open a Portal and strode through, anger resonating from every aspect of his posture.

"So you are my keeper today?" I asked him. I wasn't expecting a response.

"Keeper?" he queried. "No, I am no Keeper. There has been no Keeper in generations." The way he said it implied to me that my naming him as Keeper had some deeper meaning. He came to kneel by the water and splash some on his face. He drank deeply and cast a coin into the water.

"Tribute for the Naiad," he said at my curious expression. The coin fell into the reeds and was gone. I thought I saw a flicker of movement. Perhaps the hand that had grasped mine had belonged to this Naiad. "She lives in the water, in all water." He smiled. "She saved my life when I fell in the river as a child. I fell and hit my head. She breathed for me until my Mother came." I thought of the green face that had breathed for me at the waterfall. I thought of the hand and face that I had just seen.

"May I pay tribute too?" I told him. "I would like to, but I have no coin."

He smiled up at me and he rose to his feet. "It need not be coin. My Father works metal so coin is appropriate for me. You can choose to give whatever feels right for you." He shrugged and walked to the edge of the trees. He leaned against the rough bark of a tree trunk there and waited. He was the most unobtrusive guard I had yet seen. I knelt beside the stream and I dipped my hands into the water. I scooped up the crystal clear liquid and splashed my face with it. I took my wet fingers and explored the tender patch at the back of my head. It was fading and would not swell. I pulled the beaded thong from my hair and ran wet fingers through it. I had chosen the beads myself and threaded the leather with them. The thong was becoming dark with the wet from my hands. Some of the beads were carved wood and some were polished gemstones. There were a few strands of my hair trapped around it. I hesitated, looked back over my shoulder. But there was no flaring Portal. My guard was still leaning on his tree but he was whittling on a small piece of wood. He paid me little attention. I turned back to the water. The sun shone on it and the sparkles thrown up fragmented my sight. I held out the thong. I let it dangle from my fingertips. Ametsam wouldn't even notice it was gone. I lowered it to the water still expecting nothing to happen.

When her green-skinned hand eased from the reeds to take it I was surprised. I don't know why I was surprised. I had seen her twice before. Her head came free of the surface of the water that time. She stayed in the reeds, close to the edge where I knelt. She cradled the thong in her hand as I released it.

"You would gift me with this?" she asked, her voice as soft and musical as the water in which she lived.

"I would," I replied. "If it pleases you to accept my simple gift?" I added. Her hair hung wet and dripping around a delicate face. A soft, green sheen adorned her skin and emerald eyes gazed at me until I lowered my face from her.

"It pleases me." That soft musical voice spoke again and there was a touch. I saw her hand before it touched me. Her fingers barely brushing the skin on my chin as she eased my face up again to look at her. "But I do not wish to keep this thing of yours." She held my focus with her unblinking gaze. "You do not belong here yet. You have business unfinished in your own world and you wish to return there." I know I gaped like a stranded fish then because she laughed. "I do not read your mind. Nor do I watch or listen to you. I simply see your aura. Everything is written there. You are pulled back to your own world and he holds you here." I nodded, unable to speak. My mouth was suddenly dry. The Naiad held out cupped hands. My beaded thong lay curled there. As I watched, her hands filled with water and the leather was soaked. "This was made of the earth. It was wrought by the hands of woman. Now I fill it with the water of my body. It will bind us in a way that not even Ametsam will guess." She intoned these words like a prayer. "Take this my gift to you and heed my words." She held out her hands and I took back my thong, rebinding it into my hair. It still dripped with water and wet rivulets ran down my neck. She smiled at that.

"Thank you," I stammered to her. I could sense this was a huge gift from her.

"You are welcome," she replied. She took my hands and I felt water well up in her palms and wash over my skin. She sought and found my eyes and she stared deep into the very heart of my soul. "If you can find a Nexus of power to ground and focus you then you can find your own way home. There is a power in you. You can't yet use it as he does but it is there." She searched my incredulous face and her smile was gentle. "I know," she said. "You do not believe it. Then I will say this to you. Find the place and the moment at which you first stepped into this world and you will find your nexus. You will find your power there. I will help if I can but I can only be where there is flowing fresh water. I can escape the water for a short time but it costs me dearly. If you have need of me then soak the trinket." Her eyes darted beyond my shoulder and I followed them, turning to look behind me. My guard was still lounging against his tree. "He returns. I must leave. Remember my words. Hold them in your heart." Then she was gone, slipping away from me back into the water. By the time the Portal had flared open and Ametsam had stepped through I was standing and waiting for him. The water behind me bubbled pleasantly as it passed. My guard was by my side and managed to look suitably annoyed at his task. Ametsam dismissed him and turned to focus his attention on me. He made a snorting sound. It was a derisive noise.

"Your hair is wet," he snorted, obviously displeased.

"I felt hot so I used the water to cool me." The lie and explanation eased smoothly from my lips. "My hands were still wet when I retied my hair." He grunted dismissively.

He waved at the warrior who had been my guard. "You may return to the fortress now." Ametsam didn't even look at him as he left. He missed the short bob of the man's head towards the water. He missed that affiliation to a being other than himself. I dared to smile at my guard as he walked away and I received a smile in return. "We will return to your rooms now." Ametsam grabbed my hand hard, crushing my fingers against each other. He threw open a Portal and literally dragged me through. We stepped out in front of my fire. It had been banked while we had been out. The log basket was freshly filled. A pot of hot, steaming tea was waiting beside a platter of food on the table. He took the few paces needed to reach the table and appraised the meal there. Then motioned for me to sit and eat. He stood by the fire and watched me eat.

"Will you not join me?" I asked him.

"I have no appetite for food," he replied, his eyes never leaving me. He watched every mouthful. It became increasingly unpalatable for me to eat with him there. I could feel his eyes on me. I felt his gaze boring into me. I ate little but made sure I held a mug of the fragrant tea as I pushed my plate to one side. I sat waiting. I had no idea what he wanted or what I wanted from him.

"The stream today was beautiful," I told him. He nodded. "May we go there again?"

"Perhaps I will take you," he replied but I was suddenly not sure what he meant. There was a look in his eyes that made me shiver with a spasm of fear. He saw the terror pass across my face. He sneered at me. "Weak!" he spat. "I will teach you to obey me in all things. I am Master here. You belong to me." He folded his arms and watched the realisation of what he might do sink into my fear paralysed mind. He extended a hand and a claw beckoned me to him. I stood and went to him, of course I did. There was nothing else I could do. His hand came to the back of my neck and I felt ice form in the pit of my stomach. Whatever he wanted I could not stop. My thoughts fogged in terror. My heart almost stilled in my chest. I forgot to breathe. I felt his fingers in my hair. I felt him pull free the binding beaded leather and toss it to one side. A small part of me screamed out in fear that he had thrown it on the fire but I made no sound. His hand twined into my hair, pulling my head backwards so he loomed over me. He leaned forward and purred into my ear. "Mine."

Then the heat began. It erupted from his hands, still tangled in my hair and stabbed deep into me. The breath was locked into my lungs and I couldn't work out whether to breathe in or out. The muscles across my shoulders burned with cramped tension. But that was nothing compared to the fire racing down my spine. I couldn't think. If he hadn't been holding my hair I don't think I would have remained standing. I could barely breathe. The pain was excruciating. Whether he kept it to my back or whether he couldn't make it go further I don't know but it was my back that twisted with each muscle spasm. It was my spine that was on fire.

Just as my sight of his face blurred and darkened at the edges he let me go and I crumpled to the floor at his feet gasping as I sucked air back into my lungs. My heart was racing and every limb shook as if I had a fever. I was afraid to move in case the pain began again. His hoof poked me in the ribs and I flopped onto my back to lay there staring up at him. He stepped over me and walked from the room. I lay there with my head resting on the cold stone of the hearth until my heart settled back to normal. Only then did I gingerly try to move. I was stunned to discover there was no residual pain. There was a slight stiffness from the cramping but nothing more. I moved very carefully nonetheless to avoid it flaring again. Exhausted I crawled into my bed and tried to sleep. It was almost impossible. I listened for every creak, every sound that might mean he was back. So I lay curled into the quilted bed spread and rested but I didn't sleep.

Late that night he came. It was dark but I still lay awake. I heard the keys in the door and I curled tighter. I listened to him clipping across the floor to my bedroom. I refused to open my eyes to see him standing there. I hugged my knees to my chest even as I felt the weight on my bed. The warmth of his breath on my cheek made me curl tighter. The delicate rake of his finger along my neck sent waves of red hot pain down my spine again and I arched in reflex, opening to him.

"I plant the seed," he growled from above me. "I plant my seed and it will grow in you. You are no longer my Consort. But you will still bear my heir." He was done swiftly but once wasn't enough. Afterwards I lay there bruised and aching and still I refused to open my eyes until I had heard him leave the room, until I heard the door shut and the key turn. Only when I had heard those things did I move. I curled into a ball, wrapped into the quilted bed spread and I shook. I wept and I shook. At some point I got up. I went to find the beaded leather thong and I took it back to my bed. I clutched it in my tight fist so hard that my fingernails cut deep into my palm. I held it to my heart like a child clings to a teddy bear. Eventually I must have slept. I remember waking to see the sun coming weakly through the crystal light well. I remember stifling a cry as I heard the door open.

*Lily plunged her hands into the warm, dark soil and groped about for the potatoes she knew were there but couldn't see. Her eyes were not focused and she worked by touch alone. The sun beat warm on her back. The soil still dark and damp from last night's rain. The smell of warm soil came flooding up to her and she smiled as her searching fingers found the harvest. The limp leaves lay on the earth next to the garden fork and a pile of potatoes and carrots rested in a bucket. She heard the gate open and then close again, the catch bouncing before it latched properly.*

"Put the kettle on, Kate!" she called in greeting, without looking round. A wordless laugh confirmed her guess. Lily rocked back onto her heels and brushed the worst of the dirt from her hands. She eased herself slowly to her feet and took the bucket of vegetables up to the house. As Lily came through the door, Kate was organising mugs and tea.

"Is it all true?" Kate asked quietly.

"Yes." Lily put the bucket of veg down by the door. "As far as I know, I have no reason to doubt it."

"But why didn't she tell me?"

"I don't know." Lily washed her hands under the kitchen tap. "She meant to, she wanted to."

"I would have understood." Kate stirred the tea and handed a mug to Lily.

"I know, and I think she knew that too." Lily threw a grin over her shoulder as she went back out of the door and into the garden. "Come and help with weeding." Kate caught up and the two women pulled weeds and nattered the rest of the afternoon away.

# 7. Do what you have to.

*Kate bustled round the kitchen. Sausages sizzled and spat under the grill while potatoes bubbled furiously in a pan on the hob. Tom and Cameron peeled and sliced carrots before throwing them into a pot of water.*

*Anger and pain boiled as the dinner bubbled.*

*He'd raped her. Kate had heard it said, she'd been told, but somehow this made it very real. This was like Sam whispering the story in her ear. The more she read, the more Kate understood how hurt Sam had really been. The damage was far deeper than mere bruises.*

*Kate smiled over towards Jack, who was colouring with the girls. The three heads bent over the pages intent on pencils and crayons.*

*Only after the children had retreated to bed and Jack was tinkering with his car in the garage could Kate pick up Sam's manuscript again.*

It wasn't him. It was breakfast. I lay there, shaking until the door closed again. Then I lay there a bit longer, straining my hearing to be certain. Then I felt ashamed that I had let this happen. I had been so stupid. I know I wept. I sobbed those silent tears that pour down your face and drip into whatever is underneath. The aching numbness filled my chest until it was about to burst. Finally I got myself under enough control that I could get off the bed and go to the door. I pulled on the deep green dress but didn't bother dressing properly. I peered into the other room and saw food on the table. It was nothing like the food I had been offered up until then. There was bread but it wasn't warm, it wasn't even particularly fresh. There was butter but it had the look of old. The water was at least fresh and clean. I drank deeply before I tried the bread.

At least it wasn't stale. It was the last of yesterday's bread by the taste and feel of it, but it wasn't stale. The butter smelled rancid so I left it alone. So I breakfasted on bread and water. My mind raced blindly around the space where I avoided thinking about what he had done and what it meant. My skin remembered every detail, my body remembered. But my mind shied away. I realised I was still clutching my beaded leather thong in one hand so I absent-mindedly bound it into my hair.

As I finished my last mouthful of bread the door was flung open. I raised a cup of water to drink but had it dashed from my hand. Two armed warriors burst in and grabbed me roughly.

"What is it?" I tried to talk with them but received only a cuff to my head to silence my voice. "What's wrong?" I asked again. This time the cuff was hard enough to make me reel and I sagged in their grip. "At least let me get dressed?" I begged as the world swam around me. One of them let go and I came close to falling. In a moment he was back and he was holding a random selection of my clothing. He took a firmer grip on my arm, twisting it behind me painfully. I was propelled along corridors which became darker and dirtier as we went. I felt we moved away from the sunlight and I was petrified. They dragged me down a steep and slippery flight of steps and I stumbled more than once. Each time I was mercilessly hauled back to my feet and made to continue. It seemed like hours, but it was only minutes later that we arrived at a door. This was a depressingly scary door. It was wood, as all doors in the fortress were wood. It was stained dark and looked like it would be slimy if I could have reached out and touched it. One of my captors kicked at the door and it creaked open. It opened into whatever room it hid. They pushed me in with a shove which sent me sprawling to my knees. I knelt there, the damp seeping into my knees and I felt the bundle of clothing hit my back. As I turned to look behind me the door slammed shut and I heard bolts being drawn across. I got to my feet and reached for the clothes they had thrown in for me.

    They had thrown in a few grubby discarded garments. So I had the deep green dress I was still wearing, some woollen leggings, a tunic and a warm cloak at least. My feet were bare and feeling the slimy damp ease its way between my toes. I took off the dress and pulled on the leggings and tunic thinking they might keep me warmer. I wrapped the cloak round me as well and then I took a look about my cell. Now you know I am about five feet nine inches tall. I used that to guess at the room being a cube of about seven or eight feet on each side. The door was set into the middle of one wall and there was a small barred window towards the top, just about at the height for a tall man to look through. I gripped the bars in my hands and tried to see out but all I could see was the corridor that brought me here. There was light in that corridor so some did trickle into my cell. It was still frighteningly dark in there. I tentatively reached out my hand to the wall. It was cold and damp but not wet. The air smelled damp and musty. As my eyes adjusted to the gloom I started to take in my small world. Along one wall was a wooden platform which seemed to serve as a bed. There was a large sack filled with straw that I assumed was a mattress and two blankets. They at least smelled clean and were dry. The straw in the sack smelled fresh. There was no other source of light, only the small grill in the door. I folded the dress and placed it on the bed. I could use it as a pillow later. There was a bucket at the end of the bed which I assumed was for either washing or for using as a toilet. It was empty.

    I slowly realised there was a noise in the background. I could hear water. It wasn't dripping, nor was it truly running but I could hear water. I sat on the bed and let my eyes finish adjusting to the darkness and shadows. My hair was coming loose from having been cuffed as I had been dragged here. So I finger-combed it relatively tangle free and rebound it. The feel of the beads and leather was somehow reassuring in my hands and my hair was off my face.

    I sat there and felt numb. I couldn't work out where it had all gone so horribly wrong. I had no idea what I had done to deserve such treatment. But I was so certain it was somehow my own fault. I was so sure that if I learned and did the right things, said the right things, he would let me come back. Give him time, he's just angry, he'll get over it, is what I told myself. I told myself that he would come for me. I convinced myself that this was all a mistake and it wouldn't be long until I was released. So I huddled there with my legs drawn up under my cloak and I waited. How much time passed was impossible to tell. The light from outside my door never wavered. The sun didn't rise and set. There was no day and there was no night. I slept but I have no idea how long. Once I saw a face at the bars but I didn't know them and they didn't speak to me.

I wrapped the blankets round me as well as the cloak so I might feel a little warmer. The shivers I felt shudder through me were more from stunned fear than from actual cold. It might have been hours, it might have been days. I had been fed more than once and given water to drink. I had been left in the clothing I had. Ametsam had not come. Left alone with only my thoughts for company I felt my sense of time and reality slipping. The damp in the cell had gotten worse and the floor was now slick with slippery cold water. The trickle I could hear was now a permanent fixture and I was convinced I had been put in this particular cell so it could drive me out of my mind.

I tried to keep my thoughts from spiralling out of control by using a series of silent affirmations, mantras if you like. I told myself I would get home to see you again. I would tell you how I felt. I promised myself that we would raise our children together. I resolved that my birth did not matter, that my parents were the ones who had raised me regardless of any blood link. These affirmations were what kept me from going completely insane in those long days. I am sure it was days. I lay curled on the hard wooden bed with my back against the cold stone wall. The chill from the stone leached my body heat until I was past even shivering.

Then one day, shortly after they had fed me, I heard those distinctive footsteps approaching along that dark corridor. I felt my body curl itself tighter around the knot of blanket I had bunched into my stomach. I heard the whimper escape from my throat. Despair washed through me. He had total control now. He owned me and could use me however he wished. I dreaded what he might do next. He would see that his heir was not secure in my belly, he would know and he would do it again. I forced myself to sit up and throw aside the blankets and cloak before the door opened to reveal him.

"Sam." He curled his lip in that now-familiar cruel leer as he stepped into the tiny room, filling and dominating it. I managed to look him in the eye from where I sat. While I remembered my own humanity he could not win, not completely. He reached out his thick arm and clawed hand, offering it to me. With a supreme effort of will I reached out my own hand and allowed him to grip it and pull me to my feet. His hand was dry and warmer than my own. His skin felt more snake-like than ever. He gently caressed my hand as I stood there. He didn't release me and I struggled to keep the shivers, now of revulsion, from running through me.

"You will join me for dinner." His deeply powerful voice reverberated in the small cell. "Come." It was a command. I had no choice but to obey him. He led me from the cell and out into that pale light. I was confused. He was being nice, courteous. He was still firmly in control but I was expecting more violence, more abuse, not a command to eat a decent meal. Still I would take the chance at proper food while it was on offer. I stilled my tongue and remained silent knowing that if I questioned him it would likely lead to a triggering of his anger again. I wasn't prepared to risk that. I was terrified of what he might be capable of. I watched him warily as he led me away from my cell, waiting for a blow that didn't come, waiting for the burn of magic that would start that excruciating pain. But the pain didn't come. The anticipation was somehow worse. We came to an open door. This was not my old rooms. He stood back and allowed me to enter before him. I stepped in warily. The room was opulent. The floor was covered with thick rugs. Rich tapestries hung on the walls. There was an enormous hearth which contained a blazing fire. I moved towards it to try and ease the chill from my bones and joints.

I flinched when he came to my side and reached for my face. But his hand coolly cradled my cheek with a shocking tenderness. I stayed silent. I knew that any sound he dragged from me would be a victory. I watched him as he examined me coldly.

"You are dirty," he said at last. "You will bathe." This statement was delivered in calm tones and brooked no argument. He pushed me towards a light almost translucent screen that didn't quite hide the hot steaming tub of scented water. He followed me and I tensed as his hands worked to remove my clothing. He was gentle, almost tender but I still twitched and flinched every time he touched me. I was unwilling to stop him for fear of his strength and his anger. I shivered and told him I was just cold.

"I can wash myself," I mumbled to him.

He grinned then, his mouth curving into that sneer I had become used to. "I am sure you can," he purred. "Naiad will assist you." I felt his eyes burn over my nakedness as his gaze raked up and down my body. He stepped aside to reveal the lithe green form of the Naiad. He turned and walked to the other side of the screens leaving us in a semblance of isolation and privacy.

The Naiad held soap and cloths for washing and she smiled as I dipped a hand into the water. It was deliciously hot after the dank chill I had existed in. I gingerly lowered myself into the tub with a little encouragement and assistance from the Naiad. I submerged as far as I was able and let my aches slowly relax. She stood at the side of the tub and handed me soap and cloths as I needed them but she never allowed her own flesh to touch the water.

"I came for you," she whispered. "I need to get back into my own water and he knows it, but I can be here for a time." I looked closely and saw for the first time how dry and cracked her skin looked.

"Will this water help?" I asked softly. She nodded. "Naiad would you please help me wash my back. I can't reach it properly." I asked her in a normal tone deliberately so he would be aware. She gratefully reached into the water and I felt it shiver as she did. I watched as the skin on her arms soaked in the wet and became whole again.

"Thank you," she breathed and she took up a cloth and gently wiped my back and shoulders. I felt her hands on my skin as she kneaded away the knots that were threatening to cramp instead of relax. Her touch was soft and warm and I felt myself actually begin to enjoy it. I allowed myself that luxury for a few minutes. I relaxed in the simple companionship and the warmth of touch of someone who cared.

"You are the same Naiad aren't you?" I asked. I had to be certain. I had to hear it. I felt her nod rather than answer. "Both times?" I persisted.

"Yes." Her almost silent response was a reassurance. "There are a few who oppose him and would help get you free. But we must tread carefully. He made sure the last to oppose him was no more." There was a pain in her tone that left no doubt that she meant he had killed the person or people she was speaking about. "There, you are clean and I hope a little less tense." She came round to face me again and she wiped her wet hands on her face. I watched the liquid soak into her skin before I stood and allowed her to wrap me in a soft, warm towel.

"Naiad, would you please dispose of this water, it is filthy." Again I raised my voice a little so he would hear while waving her towards the warm water. I stuck my head round the edge of the screen to see him sitting by the fire with a large glass of wine in his hand. "Ametsam?" I called softly. He raised his head and looked at me. He nodded his approval at my new cleanliness. "My clothes are soiled," I told him. "Are there other garments here you wish me to wear?" I heard the Naiad easing water over herself as quietly as she could. She would gain some relief from it at least. He smiled and stood.

"There are clothes there for you," he laughed. "They are on the chair behind the bath." I turned to look and there was a wooden chair with fabric thrown over it. It was, predictably, a long dress; impractical but beautiful. He had excellent taste in clothing at least. It was pale linen and very simply cut but it would drape incredibly well on my frame. I loudly asked the Naiad to help me while I waved her back to the water. I wanted to give her as much time with her element as I could. She was now sitting in the water. I hoped she would be able to get out before he saw or that he would not be angry with her. I dreaded bringing his anger down on anyone else. I breathed a sigh of relief as she stepped from the water as I pulled on the dress and settled it on my shoulders. She brought a brush and bade me sit on the chair. I felt the brush move through my hair and her deft fingers pulled it to bind it back from my face. She leaned over my shoulder.

"Do you have the beaded leather?" she asked.

"I do." I pointed to my dirty discarded clothing. "It's on there." She left my side to fetch it and I saw her dip it into the water and rub it to shift the dirt. She cradled it in her hands and I saw the water flow over it.

"It is renewed," she told me. "If there is water where you sleep then leave this where the water moves. I will try to come to you. I do not know if I can, but I will try." She wove the leather into my hair, stepped round to check my appearance and smiled her approval. Her wet hand cradled my cheek and her face was full of concern. "We will try. We will do our best to get you home." With her words sitting in my heart like balm I walked round the screens to face him. His eyes roved and he licked his lips.

"Please be seated and comfortable." He waved me to the table which was set with fine food. The bread steamed gently next to a tureen of delicious smelling stew. The tureen was full of liquid rich with flavour and thick with vegetables, herbs and meat. The smell alone made my mouth water in anticipation. I resisted the temptation to simply grab the food and stuff myself. I knew he would hate that and at the moment he was smiling. I wondered if this meant he had relented and I was back in favour for a time. I hoped so. It might mean a chance to escape. So I sat with him and tried to act like I was enjoying it. He ladled thick, rich stew into a bowl and he broke a piece of bread for me. He poured wine and the fragrance reminded me of autumn berries. It was a rich plum red and glowed with the flicker of flame reflected in its depths. He had lit the room with a multitude of candles. Some of them were scented. I forced myself to relax as we ate in silence. I would let him begin any conversation. He watched every mouthful I took. His focus on me was unnerving and I found myself sliding my eyes from his intense gaze.

"You have no need to fear." When he spoke I jumped. "I was angry at your inability to conceive an heir. I acted impulsively. For that I must apologise." He sounded like he meant it but I was suspicious.

"I accept your apology," I told him. "Maybe we can just start from here?" I tried to believe he was sincere but I knew he was not.

"I would have you back at my side," he told me. It wasn't where I wished to be but it had more potential, more scope to get home. "But you anger me with your weakness and I still have no heir to pass the power to." He sounded serious. But I knew I couldn't give him what he wanted. I would have to try and think of something to distract him from that.

While we had been eating and before we started talking, the Naiad had cleared away the bath and the water.

"Ametsam," I began and he was all attention. "I have felt very alone here." He nodded, seeming to understand. "I am away from my home, my children, and the life I knew. I have no companion, no friend to speak with. Perhaps that is part of the problem?"

"Go on." He was listening. He was actually listening.

"If I could have a constant person to be with then perhaps things could be different." I wasn't sure how much I dared to suggest. I knew I dared not even consider implying I could visit you and the children. "I know your warriors have other duties. Perhaps the Naiad could be here with me? I think I could like her."

"She cannot be long away from her water," he mused, but he hadn't said no yet. "But you have always liked to walk out in the open. If a warrior went with you perhaps it would be safe." His hand stroked his beard and he seemed to consider it. I held my breath. I waited and let him think it through. I tried to be still and silent. "I shall make her a gift to you," he finally announced. I tried to keep the relief from my face. Maybe, just maybe he would let her stay long enough that she could help me. "She can make sure you are where I wish you to be. She can make sure you are dressed as I wish you to be. She can teach you what I wish you to know of your life here. Perhaps she can help you discover a way to bear my seed to fruition." I doubted that in all honesty. I firmly believed by then that he and I were more like cat and dog in our genetics and no amount of trying or forcing would produce the pregnancy he said he desired. "I will inform her of her new duties in the morning," he rumbled in his deep voice. "But this evening it shall be just you and I once again. I am Master of this realm. I control everything here. I tell each living thing its place. From the tiniest seed to the tallest tree, each knows their place only if I tell them. The birds, beasts and fish live where I command them. I am at the core, the centre of it all. I see and I am. I touch and it is mine."

As he spoke the power visibly swelled within him. This was a danger time. Now was the moment I needed to run. But I didn't. Pinned to my chair in sheer terror I sat and watched it come. The light crept from his fingers and curled in his palms. Delicately he wove it into a mobile amoeba. The shape shifted as he moulded it. It was bright, sharper and brighter than the soft glow of the candles. It held me, mesmerised by the swirling patterns within the amorphous mass in his hands. I felt the back of the chair press into my skin as I tried to retreat. I couldn't look away to see my knuckles white on the edge of the table. My heart pounded as if I had been running. The sweat pooled cold and trickled down my back. His eyes were on me, owning me but mine were on the light. He brought it to me. He held it in front of me.

"Do you know what I am able to do with this?" he asked so softly I barely heard him. I shook my head slightly, unable to tear my panic-stricken gaze from that physical manifestation of his magic. "Whatever I wish." He breathed into my ear. I felt the warmth of him there, he was that close. What he did next I am still not sure. I haven't tried to recreate it and I don't know where to start. But in a blink he and I were somehow inside his swirling light and still outside it at the same time. I felt nothing. I'm not even sure I was breathing. It was silent. In front of my eyes I watched as my memories of my life as your friend were played out as if on a cinema screen. I saw you as you were that night in the pub. You were laughing, a little drunk. Your eyes danced and it sliced my soul to see you. I saw my children, Tom trying to get too close to the fire, Susan sleeping. I loved to watch her sleep. I saw you and Jack on your wedding day. I saw Lily waiting for us in the coffee shop. I could just feel you by my side as we walked towards her. She looked up and waved. I know you went on ahead to get drinks. I remember that day so very well. It was the first time we had met up with Lily, the day our friendship cemented. I felt the connection between the three of us as clear as if it were tangible. The three witches. I heard her voice. "When shall we three meet again?" Her words were followed by your laughter.

Then the bubble burst. The light went out and I fell from my chair, gasping for breath, dragging in huge lungfuls of air. My vision was blurred and my ears hissed. Through that I heard him laugh, I thought I heard him hiss, Lilith, but I wasn't certain. His voice boomed in my stunned silence.

"I can do anything I wish. Anything I desire is within my grasp." He laughed and it wasn't pleasant. "I am Master here and I tell you your place in my realm." He bent and took hold of my arm. I reflexively pulled away from him, crawling across the floor in fear. My mind was still reeling from his brutal violation of my memories. I knew he had seen and felt all that I had. His hand flashed out and sent me sprawling onto my face. "I show you what you wish to see and you cower in fear?" The contempt in his voice was plain. "Get to your feet and face me!" He demanded as his caught the neck of my dress and roughly hauled me to my feet. I stood in front of him, swaying slightly.

"The sheer power dazed me," I told him honestly. "I am but awed and stunned by it. In the world I left there was no such power. Anyone who claimed to use magic was derided as foolish. You have shown me so little of what your power can do, I was unprepared." He seemed to accept that although I winced at the frown that passed across his features as I spoke of magic being derided as foolish. But it passed as I steadied myself. He reached out to touch me and I let him.

I lived within his rooms for the next few days. The next morning the Naiad brought my breakfast and calmly told me she was to be my companion, that the Master had decreed it to be so. I thanked her and invited her to join me for my morning meal. She declined, but sat with me while I ate. She looked better for having had access to the bath water the night before but her skin was still dry. I knew she needed to get back to her stream as soon as possible but I suspected I would not be able to leave the fortress for some days yet.

"I am to remain at you side," she informed me coolly and formally, leading me to think we were overheard. "We are to remain in these rooms today as Master Ametsam may wish to call on you later. He leaves his advice that you would look well in the purple dress and that he prefers your hair to be unbound." Her green eyes held mine as she spoke. I flicked my glance over her shoulder to where the door stood ajar and I could see the burly form of a warrior standing there. She inclined her head in agreement with my raised eyebrow.

"That suits me well, Naiad," I responded, trying to sound as light as I could. "Perhaps you could ask for some fresh bathing water to be brought so I can wash. Maybe some scented oils. I'm sure you know the ones Master Ametsam prefers." She grinned at my overly loud speech. The expression lit up her face.

"I shall do as you request Respected Consort." She clearly struggled to keep he grin from her voice. "I shall go now and see if there is anyone to ask." She rose and went to the door. I heard her talking to the guard there. She called for warm bathing water and cold spring water for a hurt I had received in a fall. I frowned a little at that. I heard her list the scents I knew he liked and then she came back to the table.

"Hurt?" I frowned. "I am not hurt."

"I know," She reassured me. "But I need cool water for the effect to last for any length of time and your cheek is red. It does look like you hit it on something." I recalled his hand sprawling me onto my face and I thought I could easily have injured my cheek then, or when I fell from the chair. I raised my hand to it and it was a little tender. I finished my breakfast slowly. My stomach was a bit delicate. The poor sustenance of the days in the cell followed by the rich meal the night before had left me feeling heavy and bloated. As I pushed back, sated, the bathing water arrived. The Naiad saw to the tub being filled and she selected the oils she would add in later. Then the cool spring water came. It was a large jug and condensation stood on its surface. She took that and the cloths that came with it and carried them behind the screens where the bath waited for me.

Later that day I declared a preference for drinking clear spring water and she arranged for fresh to be brought each day. It was a small subterfuge but it gave me pleasure to know we deceived him in that small way.

*Kate smiled. But the smile was laced with sadness. The whole thing was so painful to read but it explained so many things.*

*Kate looked at the pile of papers and realised she was over half way through. She flicked to the final page, a bad habit but one she did whenever she picked up a book.*

*Besides, Kate knew how this ended. She had been there as Sam burst from the oak tree and been there through the ensuing months before Sam had decided to stay away from them and then Kate had been there when Sam had finally been brought home to rest.*

*Even then, even at her funeral, that other place couldn't leave them alone. Kate put down the manuscript and sagged in her chair. With Lily's magic gone and Sam dead it all felt so unreal.*

# 8. Discovered

"It's open!" Kate's voice called from inside the house.

    Lily pulled open the kitchen door to see Kate sweeping the kitchen floor. "Time for a cuppa?." Lily grinned at her friend. "You can put that down." Lily stepped round the table and gently took the broom from Kate's hands. She leaned it against the wall beside the back door and turned to look at Kate before turning the kettle on.

    "That bad?" Lily called over her shoulder. Kate hunched over the table, shoulders tense. Lily frowned in concern. She took the mugs over, sat in the chair next to Kate and gently laid an arm *over her friend's shoulders. Kate leaned her head onto Lily's shoulder and she shook as the tears poured. Lily held her until the sobbing began to subside. Then she pulled her arm away to push the hot mug into Kate's hands. Kate looked up and smiled weakly.*

*"I'm sorry. Thank you," Kate whispered. She sipped at her tea. "He was such a bastard."*

*"Yes, he was." Lily nodded.*

*Kate stared. She didn't want to understand.*

*"I told you, Ametsam could wield the magic in subtle ways and he was a charming, attractive man," Lily continued slowly. "If he'd not held onto the magic and let it change him, I think he could have been a good man. I wonder if he could have been saved, like Hiann was saved." Kate nodded. Lily reached out and took Kate's hand. "I can't go back and change anything, I wish I could. What Sam and I are able to do, were able to do, is like holding a surgeon's scalpel. You can do so much good with it, but the potential for harm is huge too and sometimes it's better to just put it down."*

*Kate murmured softly, "Is it permanent? Will your magic ever come back?"*

*Lily shrugged. "I don't know. I don't think so, and I don't want it back."*

"The Naiad is becoming sick," I told him after about a week. "She needs to go back to her stream now." He had come to our rooms for the midday meal and I knew he would be back in time for the evening meal. My time locked in that tiny cell had left me wary and suspicious of anything he said or did. But he had been only charming and solicitous. He was with me for most meals and for a large portion of each day. At the beginning I would have relished the attention. Now I dreaded it. My days felt like he was watching me, restraining me. The door to the rooms was never locked but there was always a guard at the entrance. They were never to leave their post and I lacked the confidence to dare to go out alone.

He drained the glass he was holding. "Sick?" he queried. "How sick?"

"She is sick at heart," I told him. "Her skin cracks and I can find nothing that will relieve it now. She tells me she should be visiting her own stream every few days. May she please be excused from her duties for a day to do so?" I purposefully didn't suggest that I join her on this day out. I didn't want to argue with him or trigger his anger and he didn't seem to want me to leave the fortress. I was petrified that he suspected that I planned to try to escape. So I chose my words and time carefully and hoped to gain some time and healing for the Naiad. "She has become important to me," I told him and I watched his face change. He had been distracted until then. The emotion that washed across his features in response to my words was frightening. He sneered at my caring for a naiad and I feared for her. I was concerned he would use it to isolate me again. Then he seemed to think about the implications.

"It is good you have a companion," he said, "I hope you will feel more at home here now. This *is* your home. You do realise that?" I nodded, my voice sticking in my throat. This was not my home. It had become a prison and he was my jailer. He laid a possessive hand on my arm and I stopped myself from pulling away. I could tolerate his attentions until I managed to get away from him.

I waited again. I sat there with his hand on my arm and I waited.

"I shall send her to refresh herself tomorrow," he finally announced. "She can accompany us as we walk and there is no reason we should not walk to her mother stream." He smiled gently as if he offered me a magnificent gift. The blow was almost physical while the prospect of the outside, of fresh air was enough to bring a returning smile to my face. "You may inform her if you wish."

"I shall." I managed to keep my voice even as I replied. "Will I see her this evening?" The Naiad was often not present when Ametsam was in our rooms. I didn't know if that was her choice or his instructions.

"No." His voice was seductive, purring. "I wish to keep you for myself this evening." The ownership laced into his tone made me feel nauseous. He ran his clawed fingertips along the line of my jaw. I shivered and he leered. "You will bathe and prepare yourself for my return this evening. I will arrange for water and scents for you." He raised my hand to his face and kissed my palm with cold lips. He pressed my hand to his cheek and then turned his head into it. His tongue flicked out and teased the skin there in the centre of my palm before he released me. He strode from the room without looking back. The door swung behind him but did not completely close. I could see the broad back and glint of metal that came from the now ever-present warrior guard. I heard a voice and then another. I listened to his footsteps recede as he paced down the corridor.

Then I laid my head on my arms and allowed myself to weep. Despair flowed through every pore and my tears provided no relief. Even though the door was left open in these rooms I was still just as much a prisoner as I had been in the cold, dark cell. I knew the cell was always a possibility if I couldn't keep him happy and believing that I was willing. It was a hard act to keep up when revulsion washed through my stomach and my gorge rose every time he touched me.

She brought breakfast in the morning as usual. I was up and dressed comfortably in warm trousers, boots and an embroidered linen blouse in a tunic style. It was practical while being feminine enough to satisfy him. She looked tired and somehow diminished as she laid out the food she had brought. As always I invited her to join me and, as always, she refused.

"We are to walk out today," I told her as I ate slowly. She looked up from where I had asked her to sit. She would have been tidying up while I ate but she appeared to be so very tired. So I had bidden her join me and keep me company at least. She had our jug of clear spring water and was resting her hands in it.

"I'm not sure I can." Her voice was barely louder than a whisper. "I am failing. This water is no longer enough to sustain me." Her head sagged to her chest. "I am dying, Respected Consort. I am dying."

I reached out my hand and placed it on her arm. "Naiad," I called softly and her head lifted. "He has said we will walk to your Mother stream. I am taking you home to replenish yourself." She smiled and the news seemed to revive her a little.

"May I use your bathtub?" she asked.

"Of course you can," I told her and watched as she clutched the jug of spring water to her and walked around the screens. After a short pause there came the sound of pouring water and I knew she cascaded the water from the jug over herself. When she returned the jug was empty and dry. She was a little more restored. Her skin was smooth once more and the cracks had gone but the sheen and vibrant life had not returned.

"I will not be able to come back to the fortress today," she informed me calmly. "In order to replenish and revive myself fully I must remain in my water from dusk until dawn, a full rising and setting of the moon. I shall be back in the morning. Unless you wish to wait there with me for the night?"

"I would gladly wait with you Naiad," I replied slowly. "But Master Ametsam will be accompanying me and I think he will insist I return here for the night." I smiled at her. "But I will suggest it to him. He may appreciate a night away from the stresses of his rule here." She nodded and then moved to clear away the breakfast things. As she took them from the room he appeared in the doorway. She had to wait for him to fully enter the room before she could leave.

"Greetings, Respected Consort," he said formally.

"Greetings, Master Ametsam," I replied, just as formally. Some days he liked to stay formal and I had to be careful what I said to him and how I phrased it. "Does it still please you that we go walking today?" I asked tentatively. "I had hoped to revisit the Naiad's stream. She has told me more of its history and I am intrigued."

"It does indeed please me," he boomed. "I have had a lunch prepared for us. Your Naiad will be given it to bring back here when she returns from the kitchens." He walked across to the table and sat opposite me. "How much do you know of naiads my Consort?"

"I know very little," I confirmed for him. "I know only what she has told me."

"She will need to be submerged in her own Mother Water for a complete moon." He was explaining exactly what she had just told me. "She must be immersed before sundown this evening and remain there until sunrise tomorrow. Otherwise she will not reap the full benefits of the healing properties there. She will not replenish sufficiently to return to you."

"Is that so?" I pretended ignorance. "Then she must stay overnight and will have to come back to me in the morning. I do not wish to see her harmed or for her to become sicker." It was not hard to let my concern for the Naiad show in my tone and on my face. She needed this and I needed her. She was the first person who had given me any hope that I might somehow be able to make it back to you and the children. I had that glimmer of hope now and I held fast to it like someone drowning will cling to anything that floats.

He nodded seriously. "I would not have you parted from her just yet. I approve of the friendship you have formed and do not wish it harmed. You seem more rooted here in this world since I allowed the Naiad to be with you." He smiled and I couldn't miss the edge to it that spoke differently. He would use the Naiad to control me. He thought he had found another part of my life that he could use to cause me pain and gain more control. "I have arranged for my pavilion to be erected near the Naiad Mother Water so we may both be near her while she replenishes herself." He watched for my reaction and I had no idea what he hoped to see. I mustn't appear too eager or he would suspect something. I mustn't seem too grudging or disappointed or he may have cancelled the whole idea. I allowed the edge of my pleasure to show in a coy smile. It seemed to satisfy him but I knew I was on dangerously shaky terrain with him over this.

"I would appreciate spending time in the open air again," I told him carefully. "I know the Naiad will appreciate having us nearby and I am grateful for this chance to learn more of our world." I chose my words with an enormous degree of care.

The door swung open to admit the Naiad carrying a basket that was clearly a little too heavy for her. I dared not offer to help her even though I longed to just get up and take it from her. I knew I could manage heavier items better than she could. I was physically stronger but she exuded a wonderful calm that was almost infectious.

So we set off. The weakest of us carrying the load and the strongest striding ahead heedless of whether anyone could keep up with him. I was grateful that it was autumn by now. The sun would not be too hot and would not dry out the Naiad's skin before we could reach her mother water. Ametsam was garrulous as we walked. He pointed out leaves, trees, flowers, landmarks like he had done when I first stepped through into his world. I could just about let my mind drift enough to believe life could work here, maybe I didn't need to get back to you quite so badly after all. I saw a side to him I hadn't seen in an exceedingly long time. I found myself willingly taking his arm and listening with genuine interest to him as he chattered on about this wonderful realm he commanded.

He stopped suddenly as the sun was almost directly overhead. As it was autumn, the sun would never be quite overhead but this was as close as it got and meant it was noon or thereabouts. He stood stock still, statue-like although he cast his head about like a dog hunting for a scent. I looked around. There were trees as usual. The ground was covered in grass, long and wet against my legs. I felt and heard the Naiad stop beside me and I turned to check that she was coping. She was clearly tired and struggling but still I dared not lend assistance to the person he thought of as my servant rather than my companion, confidante and friend. Her eyes darted between us, between me and Ametsam. She gasped then but I think he missed it. She was reaching to take my arm when he turned to face us. His head snapped round and she dropped her hand. His eyes fixed on my puzzled face, he didn't notice the movement. At least my hammering heart hoped he had missed it. He said nothing but he locked my eyes into his burning gaze. He stepped towards me and I felt like running then but my legs were turned to stone. From the corner of my eye I saw the Naiad watching us but I was unable to look away from him.

"It was here," he whispered to me, breathless. "It was here." I must have looked confused. I had no clue to what he meant. "It was here, in this spot Sam. Don't you remember?" He gestured around us with a wild sweep of his arm and I ducked. The spell was broken and I could look away from him. I searched around but saw nothing I recognised especially. I didn't even recall walking this particular path. I told him so. "Ah but it was such a fortunate day. I came here searching for my Lilith and as I opened a window onto another world I found you instead. You sat in that soulless metal and you wept, you raged and you burned so bright it was like gazing into the sun. Here, on this grass, beneath these trees I opened that window and I saw you. I dared open a Portal. I knew Lilith wasn't there but I opened it anyway and I stepped through. We spoke for the first time there and this very spot is where I brought you through to my realm." He threw his head back and he laughed. I heard the Naiad's gasp of shock as the importance of this information seeped into me. This was the place where I had first stepped into Ametsam's world. All I had to find now was the moment. But my heart swelled in my chest at the thought that he had unwittingly given us half of the puzzle. Then, just as fast, it deflated and sank at the realisation in my mind that the moment was long gone. Time had passed, how could I find that moment at which I entered his world? The moment had gone, slipped away in my inability to stand up to him, lost in my fear. Ametsam was still speaking and I realised I had missed most of his rambling.

"I know that's where she stepped out of our realm, where she ran from me. But I didn't know where she'd gone." I assumed he was still speaking of his beloved Lilith. He swung from adoration of her to hating her with such intensity that I feared for her when he finally found her. He rested one hand on the trunk of an ancient oak tree. "But I found you. You don't have her power but you are still special to me. And you showed me so much." He swooped and curled me into his arms. I was afraid. I wasn't sure where his exuberance had come from. But my fear froze me to the spot. I could have run but this was his world, I knew I wouldn't get far. So when he lowered his face to kiss me I let him, I even returned the kiss. "Come Naiad, let me take that for you." He broke free of me and held out a hand to her. "That basket is heavy and you are sick." Her eyes flicked to me in confusion and I nodded as little as I could but she got the message. She held out the basket to him and allowed him to take it. I caught her eye again as he strode off into the trees and I shrugged. She came to walk beside me and she took my arm but I knew it was more for her own benefit than for mine.

We trailed after him for a while longer and then we stepped from the trees and she gasped in relief. This was her mother water, her home stream. Ametsam was heading for the pavilion that was already in place. There was a table and chairs in front of it and he was setting out our picnic lunch.

"Go to your water, Naiad." He waved her over to the stream. She clutched at my arm for a second before running for the water. She stepped in and sank to her neck with a look of calm easing the lines in her face. I looked between the two of them, unsure who to go to. I desperately wanted to go and kneel by the water and be there with the Naiad but I thought he would become angry if I went to her first. So I went to him at the pavilion.

He watched me make my choice and smiled his approval. I was clearly playing my part well. I looked over my shoulder to see the Naiads' face disappear beneath the surface of the water and I smiled. She would be able to heal properly now. I felt his hand on my shoulder.

"This brings you much pleasure does it not?" he asked. I nodded. "I am glad," he said and he slipped his arms around me. I leaned back against his broad chest and I felt him sigh with acceptance of my surrender. He released me after a moment and stepped away. "You will see to our food," he stated and vanished into his pavilion. I was ravenous after the long walk and wanted to give the Naiad as much time alone in her mother water as I could before I tried to go and check she was all right. So I went to the table to investigate what food he had thought to bring. The table was full of covered dishes and plates. I uncovered some of them and discovered gastronomic delights. Grinning to myself I set to revealing the rest. He emerged from the pavilion to say that all was as he had demanded. He sat at the table and I was expected to sit with him. He had positioned himself so I had my back to the stream and was unable to look for the Naiad. I told myself it was coincidence. But I didn't dare look round to see her. We ate and he told me of the day he brought me through that first Portal. That night we sat on the grass and watched the moon rise over the water. The light it cast was magical. The moon was just past full, waning now towards a dark moon. The Naiad had disappeared into the deepest part of the stream and I hadn't caught sight of her in hours. I assumed this to be a good sign.

As the night grew ever darker he took me by the hand and led me into his pavilion, where he once more planted his seed. I had grown used to it by now and fervently hoped I was right and he could not make me pregnant in his current form. I dreaded the day he chose to use the magic on a microscopic level to alter our DNA or just implant something I didn't dare let myself think about. As the sun rose so did we. The light shone through the pavilion's canvas walls creating a soft warm womb like light. I woke first and told him I was going to ask if it was acceptable to wash in the stream. He grunted and I took it for his agreement.

I left the pavilion and saw the Naiad waiting in the water. I went to her without appearing to be in too much haste. I knelt by the edge of the stream and used the cool, clean water to wash my hands and face. She rose from the water and took my hands.

"We know where," she said with her eyes fixed on mine. "We know the place where your Nexus will be. If we can find the moment then there will be a way to get you home. You will need someone on the other side to anchor the link while you go through. Is there someone?" I nodded.

"Kate," I murmured. "Kate was always my anchor."

"What day did he find you?" she asked.

I let my mind wander back. I let my memories enfold me. "It was night, the moon was full. It was raining. Autumn." I spoke slowly, allowing the full recollections to surface unhindered. "I was going to my parents. Not my birth parents, not to those who made me but to those who raised me." She watched me and listened closely. "It was autumn. The leaves were red and gold, they fell on my car. It was a day or two before Samhain. I was meant to be back in time for the party. Naiad, what was I thinking? Why did I let him take me?" I felt my face twist in desperation and hopelessness. "That moment is frozen in time. We can't find it."

"Yes we can." Her hands gripped mine and I saw water flow over them, felt it wash out the despair, felt it bring calm. "Samhain is in less than two weeks. It will be a dark moon not a full moon but that may bode well. It is most of your moment. It should work." She looked up and over my shoulder and when she spoke her voice was louder, pitched to carry. "My thanks to you. I am much replenished and will gladly accompany you back to the fortress this morning." She raised herself to look past me. "Morning Greetings Master Ametsam," she called and I knew he was there. How much had he heard? The panic must have shown on my face because I felt and returned the reassuring squeeze of her hands before she let go. "I trust you slept well?" she asked him as she rose from the water and stepped past me, once more the water creature I had first met.

I felt him stop and stand behind me before his hand met my shoulder as I got to my feet. "Naiad, you have served us well." His voice rumbled in my ear and he gripped my shoulder firmly. "If you wish, you may remain here for a few days and return to the Consort's side when you are ready." I felt my stomach lurch. He had heard her words, he had heard our plan. Cold sweat pooled and ran down my back.

"I am revitalised Master Ametsam." She told him. "I am able and willing to return with you when you are ready. I await your instructions." She stood in front of us and waited for him.

"I prefer that you remain here," he growled and I heard the threat before she did. I felt his arm move and he blasted hot white fire into her. She screamed and fell backwards into the water. The clouds of steam that rose were horrifying to me. The water churned and boiled under his onslaught. He poured the power into her mother water as he held me firm, made me complicit in his action. I let him. I stood there and I didn't even try to tear myself free of his hand. I stood by him as the tears flowed down my cheeks. I was sure he killed her. He had heard us and he had killed her. He had taken the one friend I had in his realm and he had destroyed her. I thought I felt him sway a little. The stream of power stopped. It was like flicking a light switch. The water I stared at was smoking, steaming and the stench was nauseating. As the clouds cleared there were fish floating white on the surface of the water and blackened plants floated charred at the edges.

"You bastard." I heard my voice but didn't believe I had spoken the words aloud until I felt his hand collide with my head. He pulled at my tunic so I was turned to face him and he held me while he hit. Blow after blow rained down and I felt grass under my knees without knowing when I had dropped to my knees. I wrapped my arms round my head to try and protect it but the blows kept coming. He stood over me, anger flushing his face dark.

"You think you can escape me?" he spat as he shook me back to my feet. He thrust his face towards me until his nose pressed against mine. His hands were pinning my wrists behind me and he pulled me close to him. With one hand he held me tightly while he opened a Portal with the other. He dragged me through not caring if I kept my feet under me. My legs shook and I don't think I could have remained standing unaided. I couldn't see clearly and I wasn't sure if his blows had hurt me to the point of passing out or if panic fogged my sight.

"I'm sorry," I whispered. "I'm so sorry. I tried. Oh Gods, I tried." I wasn't speaking to him then but to you. I knew with crippling certainty I would never escape him alive. Only my death would release me from him and he was going to cause it. I was going to die at his hands, slowly and painfully. My arms were twisted up behind my back causing ripples of pain through my shoulders. He pulled me from the Portal outside the huge double doors of the fortress. He didn't slacken his grip or his pace. When I stumbled he hauled me back to my feet and cuffed me again making my head spin. I felt the breath suck in and out of my lungs so fast I knew I was hyperventilating. Something ran down into my mouth and I tasted blood.

He dragged me down the corridor and I knew we headed towards the cell he had thrown me in before. This time there would be no way out. He flung open the door and hurled me inside. I hit the far wall and bounced off it to fall in a heap on the floor. I lay there feeling numb as I heard the door slam and his footsteps sound fainter as he walked away.

I raised my head first and peered at the door to make sure it was shut and I was alone in there. Only when I was sure did I haul myself onto the bed and curl myself into one of the blankets that still lay there. It was darker than before, shadows pooled furthest from the door, and I was beyond afraid now, beyond terror.

I tried to work out how badly hurt I was but I couldn't separate one pain from the next. As the skin swelled and sweat began to sting I discovered new hurts, but I was fairly certain nothing was broken. I tried to sleep but I was aware of every tiny sound and I couldn't get comfortable. I couldn't see beyond his killing me. My mind played me every image after image of pain before I died. I knew that more physical beatings would drain my body and eventually he would cross that line and cause damage that was irreparable and then I would die. But what I feared was the magic. He could get into my mind and my body and make me do anything he wished. He could cause pain without injury. He could make me dance on fire like a puppet. I felt something in me snap then. It was almost a physical rip.

After a time I forced myself to sit up and hunt for the bucket that had been there before. I could hear the trickle of water again. Using my teeth I tore a strip off the bottom of my tunic and gingerly walked round the walls until I found the water. There was a distinctly wet line in one corner. I soaked the cloth and used the upturned bucket to sit on as I held the cold wetness to my face. I started with my nose and wiped away the blood as best I could. I tried to slow the swelling around one eye that was threatening to close completely. I sucked some water into my mouth and spat it out to clear the blood taste. Then I sucked in more and let it trickle down my throat. That was threatening to close too but from fear rather than swelling. My nose was still slowly leaking blood so I sat for a time with the cloth pressed there. It was bruised but not broken I decided. Sitting and dealing with myself I found a measure of stillness if not calm. I know I purposefully distracted myself from what might come next.

When I had done as much as I could without being able to see where the bruises were I returned the bucket to its place at the foot of the bed and settled back down to rest a bit if I could.

*Kate put down the manuscript. "Bastard," she whispered. "You utter bastard." She pressed the papers to her face and closed her eyes. "Oh, Sam. Why didn't you tell me? I would have listened. I would have understood."*

*The kitchen door swung open with a bang and Kate slid the papers back into the plain card folder as Jack and all four children hurtled through the door. "What's for dinner Mum?" demanded Cameron as he shed his school bag and coat onto the floor.*

*"Cameron! Pick those up and deal with them properly," Kate snapped at him. Tom rapidly salvaged his coat before it hit the floor. They came back to the table with their bags, knowing homework came before anything else in the evenings. They pulled out books and pencil cases and started work. Jack sat with them and tried to help. Under cover of the ensuing chaos Kate slid the folder into its home among the cookbooks.*

# 9. Name.

*Kate stood on the landing in the dark.*

*She could hear gentle shuffling from the girl's room. Susan had always been a restless sleeper and Hayley slept through anything, even more now they were teenagers.*

*From the boy's rooms there came low chatter and the hiss and pop of music playing quietly, they wouldn't sleep until later but they knew not to disturb anyone.*

*She stood safe in the dark and soaked up the sounds of the night. Dishes clattered and splashed in the kitchen. Jack was trying to be quiet and failing. Kate smiled, he always failed to be quiet.*

*She padded softly down the stairs and into the kitchen. Jack was washing up, elbow-deep in suds and steaming water.*

*"You don't need to do that." Kate spoke softly.*

*Jack jumped. "I didn't hear you come back down," he blushed "Was I making too much noise?" Kate stepped up to him and shook her head. She took his hands and dried them for him.*

*"Leave it," she whispered, taking his face in her hands and leaning up to kiss him, stretching up onto her toes. She felt his heart pound against her ribs as he slipped his arms round her and his warm hands lay loosely on her back. His breath on her cheek came fast and hot. Kate pulled her face away from him but left his arms round her. "I love you." She placed her palms on his chest and gently broke the embrace.*

I think I slept. Time certainly passed, but I'm not sure how much. I don't know why he stayed away but it was torture for me. I curled on the bed in terror and lost track of the time. There was no daylight to show me if it was night or day. Meals were irregular and I suspected only when someone remembered I hadn't been fed for a while. I know I lost weight. The tunic and leggings I wore hung like sacks on me and I could feel bones where there should have been padding. I think it was only a few days but it's amazing how fast the body can shed flesh when under stress and with no decent food. I know my reserves went to healing and to sustaining a constant state of near panic. I took off the beaded leather in my hair and I stashed it under the bed, tying it to the wood there.

The door swung open and a pair of armed warriors stood there. One stood filling the doorway with his hand on the hilt of his sword. The blade was loose in the scabbard and I knew could fly out and their aim was deadly when it suited them. I sat on the bed and waited. The other one took a step into the room and beckoned me. The tension in his muscles was obvious and I knew he would strike at little provocation. These men were either afraid of me or of what Ametsam would do to them. Their faces were set and cold but not angry, just unfeeling or hiding their feelings so deep I couldn't see them. They didn't tie my hands. They walked one in front and one behind me along that long, dark corridor and there was no way I could have even tried to run. Anyway, where would I go? The Naiad was dead. My hope was gone. I was unable to move my mind past that. She was gone. He had killed her and at the same time he'd killed any hope I had. I was empty, numb and my mind whirled round the image of that boiling water. Over and over I saw his hand reaching out and hurling lightening into the water. The steam rose and she died. I had no way home and no hope of finding one. I knew the time and the place where it might be possible but I hadn't the first clue as to how to make it happen, how to open a Portal.

We came to an open door. The leading warrior guard stood to one side to let me pass through the doorway. A hand in my back sent me stumbling into the room and I turned in time to see the door firmly closed behind me. I looked around the room in which I found myself. The room was large and bare. The high, vaulted ceiling should have been breathtaking but it was cold and grey. The stone slabs were freezing underneath my bare feet and leached my body's heat down into their ice. The walls were bare stone blocks. I wrapped my arms around myself in a hopeless attempt to keep in some warmth.

The room seemed empty. It felt empty, disused. There were cobwebs hanging and dust on the edges of the floor. As I looked closer I saw marks on the floor that I was suddenly certain I didn't want to see. Most of the middle of the room had been swept free of dust and there was a large hearth. Even had it been laid with a fire and had that fire been lit, the heat would not have warmed that room. The hearth was clean. No fire had burned there in days.

The pain, when it came, hit me in the small of my back. He had been standing beside the door and behind me. A single casual flick of a fingertip and a narrowly focused line of power lanced into my lower spine sending shock waves of pain through my legs. I buckled and fell hard onto my knees. The breath flew from my lungs and I knelt there gasping. I pressed my hands to the floor to steady myself and hung my head to ease the sudden dizziness. I heard him step across the stone floor, hooves clear and loud in my ears. A shove in the back sent me sprawling to lie face down on the floor. He reached down and gripped the back of my tunic as you would hold a kitten by the scruff of its neck. With one hand he lifted me from the floor and back on to my feet. Still holding my tunic he pushed his face close to mine. His grip on the fabric held it tight against my throat and I swallowed convulsively. I hung there, limp as a rag doll until his other hand came up to my throat. I flinched at the first delicate touch but did not move until his fingers curled round my neck. Then my hands flew up to catch hold of his wrist. The arm under my hands was hard as the stone floor my feet barely touched. He held most of my weight with the hand on my tunic back but the hand on my throat was tight enough to be hideously terrifying. I found my mouth dry and it felt like he was tightening his grip there, squeezing harder. His lips grazed my skin as he whispered into my ear.

"You are mine, body and soul." It was something he had told me often. He had said it when I thought everything was perfect. Those words I had valued and clung to. I was his, I belonged here. But now, in this setting, they sent ice through me. "You are the way. You will gift me with what I desire. I will wring it from you if I must." I still thought he wanted his heir and I was sure by then that what I thought he wanted was impossible. He lowered me gently to the floor. He waited until my legs could take my weight again and I stood in front of him. Defiantly I faced him. While I kept my humanity he had not defeated me completely. His hands reached out and cradled my face. His fingers stretched out on either side of my head, thumbs on my cheeks. He stroked his thumbs there. The slight curl of his lip should have warned me but it didn't.

My head exploded into pain worse than that migraine I had when I was pregnant. The heels of his hands rested under my jaw and his fingers held the rest of my head so I couldn't even scream. I felt the tears pour hot over my face. Eyes open wide, my sight of him blurred. The pain spread through my neck which cramped in agonising spasms. I heard ragged breathing and knew it was my own. I heard dull whimpering and knew I heard my own muffled voice. His cool palms were solid against my own soft flesh and held me firm. I held on to his wrists, one in either hand but they were about as moveable as bedrock. I felt my feet leave the floor and I was dangling from his hands. How long he held me there I don't know. The pain kept shooting through my head and neck until I couldn't see properly. Stabbing white hot spikes were repeatedly driven through my skull. The world went dark.

The floor pressed cold against my cheek as my eyes dragged open. I tried to lift my face from the floor but was rewarded with only a stabbing pain across my shoulders. My arms lay at my sides and I was face down on stone. I tried to see where I was but it was dark. I dragged a hand up to near my face and felt my shoulders ease a little with the movement. I dragged my other arm up and tried to lift free of the floor. I shuffled into a curl and onto my side. I waited there for the muscles to slowly settle and for the cramp to calm a bit. My head was throbbing and I felt covered in bruises.

My eyes were closed again and I was still curled on my side on the floor. I forced them open and looked around as far as I could. I was back in my cell. I had clearly passed out and been brought back here while unconscious. I lay there for a time before I felt able to move again. Then I hauled myself carefully onto the bed. Other than being stiff from lying on the floor I could find no serious injuries.

He had me dragged out to inflict pain more times than I can remember. I think it must have been every day, maybe more than once a day. He refined his technique until he could send a finely honed tendril of light to a selected area and cause whatever pain he could imagine. Sometimes he didn't use magic but he used his fists and hooves equally well. I never knew what to expect from him.

Once he had me just stand in the middle of the room while he walked round me. I don't know what he meant me to do but it left my nerves jangling. The unpredictability kept me on a knife edge all the time. I barely slept for fear and for pain.

After a few days I stopped seeing human faces at all. I saw Ametsam's blue demonic visage daily and if he didn't come to drag me from my cell himself he sent his new pet to do the job.

The creature was huge. It was not quite twice as tall as I am but so solidly built it was easily several times my bulk. It filled the corridor and had to bend to avoid bashing its head at every step. It was greyish green and covered with fine armour-like scales. It reminded me of a bipedal crocodile, brutal and just intelligent enough to be cruel while obeying orders. Its massive head rested on wide shoulders with no real neck in between. Its close-set eyes lent it an air of stupidity that I soon learned was not the case. The eyes were set above a wide flat nose that was covered with small bumps. The mouth was filled with razor sharp but dirty teeth, including a pair of long tusks that jutted up from the lower jaw. Across the chest scales and coarse bristly fur fought for dominance. Its thickly muscled arms hung from those shoulders and ended in clawed paw-like hands. For all their lumpishness those hands were capable of a fineness of touch that could elicit the most excruciating pain. Its splayed feet had three wickedly clawed toes and these made an unusually distinctive pattern on the stone floors. I could tell who was coming for me by the sound of their footsteps. It slept outside the door to my cell adding its brutish stink to the unpleasant miasma building in there.

I hadn't seen a human face in days by then and was beginning to wonder where they had all gone. I thought he had probably simply isolated me from those that seemed familiar. I hoped his abuse hadn't spread to include any who had shown me the slightest sign of familiarity or even friendship.

The Naiad's boiling stream still haunted me. It sent shivers through me every time I allowed myself to think of how she must have died. It shames me to admit it but I tried not to think of you or the children during those days. I didn't want him to know you or to be able to use you against me.

I sat on my bed with my knees pulled up tight to my chest. My feet were freezing so I had a blanket wrapped round my legs. The wet corner of my cell was getting worse and water oozed from the stones now and didn't quite run down the wall. But the cell was cold and dank now. The damp made it impossible to rest properly when he left me alone for any length of time. If I slept I woke stiff and aching. If I didn't sleep I stayed exhausted. It just added to my misery. So, I ached, I hurt and I despaired.

I had tried saving some of the bread they gave me but it went to mould within a short time. I had constant fresh water so I bathed any bruises and physical injuries and kept as clean as I could. But I couldn't wash out any of my clothing, it would never have dried and I would have frozen sitting there naked and waiting.

He stood by the door again. I swayed on my feet in the middle of that echoing space. There was a fire in the hearth this time and I tried to soak up as much dryness and heat as I could. But he had made me stand just far enough away that I could just feel the warmth but actually didn't benefit at all.

"You may go to the fire if you wish." He spoke suddenly and I startled at his voice. It was shockingly soft. I waited for the pain. My legs refused to move. "I will not have you sicken and die. Go to the fire and warm yourself," he insisted. He pulled open the door and turned away from me to speak with his pet. I was so incredibly suspicious but I did take a few steps towards the fire. I managed to get close enough to really let the heat warm me. I kept my gaze towards him, watching his every move. He folded his arms across his chest. "Your clothing is rags," he observed with a scowl. "Did no-one give you clean garments? Did you not think to ask for fresh clothing?" He made my appearance and smells my fault; he laid the blame at my feet.

"I have seen none of your warriors in days," I told him as calmly as I could muster. "There has been nobody to ask and nothing was brought." I stood with my back to the fire and let the blaze ease through me. I felt the filthy damp on my skin dry and crack. My damp and dirty hair stank as it dried and his nose wrinkled in disgust.

"I would have you clean," he announced and bellowed instructions round the door. The scaly monster appeared carrying a small tub in its arms. Water sloshed in it promisingly. While part of me was pathetically grateful for the chance to be clean, part of me dreaded what this meant. The tub was placed by the fire and was followed by the first warrior I had seen in days. He carried buckets of water. They steamed and the scent that came from them was spicy and warm. I stood aside to let him add them to the tub.

"Naiad lives."

I stared at him in disbelief. He spoke so softly as he splashed the water into the tub that I wasn't certain I had heard him. My head shot up at the words and I stared at his face. It was the man who had offered his own tribute to the Naiad in return for her saving his life as a child. My eyes flickered over to Ametsam, standing by the door looking irritated at the slowness of the task. The man in front of me let a small smile creep onto his face and he gave an almost imperceptible nod. The second bucket was lifted and, as he poured it noisily, he spoke again.

"She will tell you how that is possible when she comes. There is running water in your cell. Use the talisman she gave you. She will try to come. I will try to get you outside if I can. I dare not say more." Then the bucket was empty. With a derisive grunt he took up the empty buckets and stalked out of the room. To Ametsam he looked like a warrior disgruntled with being saddled with such a menial task.

I was alone with Ametsam and a hot bath. A year previously that would have been wonderful. Now I felt shaky and unwilling to disrobe in front of him. He stood by the door and stared at me. His arms were folded across his chest and his feet set apart. He leered at my obvious discomfort.

"You do not wish to be clean?" he demanded of me. "The water is for you, use it. Clothing is coming." He nodded to the steaming water. "Go ahead. I insist you use it." His jaw was tight and a frown had begun to crease his forehead. I stood paralysed by my indecision. I so very much wanted and needed to soak in the hot water and wash away the grime and filth as well as letting the heat ease my body. But he watched. He didn't take his eyes from me and I didn't dare ask him to. As I hesitated he strode across the room to me. He reached out his hand and literally ripped the tunic from my cowering back. I heard it hiss as it hit the flames in the hearth. "Do I have to remove your other clothing?" he snarled. I shook my head in mute denial my hands already fumbling at my leggings. I pulled them off and stepped carefully into the tub. He reached down and threw the filthy fabric onto the fire where it hissed and spat alongside the torn tunic.

He stood and watched as I scrubbed the grime from my skin. The water was soon grey and covered in a layer of scum but I was cleaner than I had been in days. I felt better for it and almost excused my own complicity in what I knew was to come next. I knew I began to wall it out, to shut myself off from the violation I expected.

I woke, naked, torn and bruised, in my cell. I was curled on my side on the bed. Someone had thrown a blanket over me but I had no recollection of getting there. I kept my eyes squeezed tightly closed but the smell and sound of trickling water was now as familiar as my own heartbeat.

"He said I would get clean clothes," I sobbed as my mind clung to the most insignificant thing that it could. The tears ran down my cheeks and soaked into the fabric covering the straw mattress. My shoulders shook and I tried to curl tighter.

A time later I unfolded my head from where it lay smothered by my arms. My neck was stiff and the incessant trickle of water was mental torture along with the damp it brought that seeped into every joint. I forced my shoulders to relax and reached under the mattress for the beaded leather thong. A shiver ran through me as my fingers touched it.

"Naiad lives." I whispered the words like a prayer and felt the edges of a smile creep across my face. "She survived him." My voice was barely more than a breath. I felt hope bloom somewhere deep inside me and the tears fell again. But this time they were tears of promised hope rather than despair. I sat up and pulled a blanket round my shoulders. "Naiad lives and I have my talisman." I clutched it fiercely to my cheek and I think I rocked as I sat there. A bundle fell into the water on the floor as I moved. I picked it up. Clean leggings and a tunic. I shot out a hand and grabbed it before it could get too wet. Whoever had put the blanket over me had put the clothes on the bed. I suspected the young man who had told me the Naiad still lived and I was grateful to him. I pulled on the tunic and leggings and then wrapped the blanket round me again. I still shook and I couldn't stop the tears flowing but I was a little warmer.

I sat huddled under the blanket until I finally stopped shivering. It seemed to take forever. The beaded leather thong was still clasped in my hand. I clung to his words. "Naiad lives. Running water. Use the talisman." I wrapped my arms round my knees and tugged the blanket tighter. The water ran freely down the wall now. The corner of my mind that was still clear wondered how they had managed that. I stepped out of my blanket and left it discarded in a crumpled heap on the bed. My bare feet touched the wet floor and I winced. It was cold and slimy now and the wet oozed unpleasantly between my toes. I pulled a face but still took the couple of steps through the puddles to reach the far side of my tiny cell.

I hugged the beaded leather to my chest, my arm curled tightly into my ribs. I reached out my other hand to tentatively poke at the wall. I was half expecting the wall to be less than solid. It was wet. Water ran down the stones in more than a trickle but less than a pour. It flowed over my fingers in a cold stream. If I pressed the edge of my hand against the wall I could pool some in my palm. I let some collect there and then lapped at it with my tongue. The water was cool and sweet. The wall was damp and slimy where the water had been running over it, steadily increasing its flow. I rocked back on my heels suddenly filled with doubt.

The young man was one of Ametsam's warriors. What if his words had been calculated to make me try this? What if I was being manipulated into betraying the Naiad and our plans? I so very much wanted to believe she had survived him but the doubt wracked me like physical pain. I scuttled back to the bed and sat there with my wet hand still dripping sweet water. I brought my hands together to rest my head in them and light flared. A small sun cradled in my palms. I was so shocked I dropped the beaded leather. I scrabbled on the slippery floor to retrieve it, unable to really believe what I had just seen. Fear washed through me. I glanced at the door. Surely the pet had seen it too. I heard its rasping breath through the door, I knew it was there. I sat back on the bed, my breath coming in short, shallow gasps. I let my head sag back to rest against the wall and steadied myself. My heart was pounding hard inside my chest.

 I went to the water and wet my hand again. Then, sitting back on the bed I brought the beaded leather onto my dripping palm. The glow flared again, bright as lightning. I took them apart, the glow faded. I wiped my hand and tried again. There was nothing. It was the water. It tasted like spring water and the way it had found its way into my cell was uncanny. Hope seeped back into my mind as the water seeped into my cell.

 I got to my feet, beaded leather gripped tight in my hand. The door was pushed open and I shot back to my bed, shoving the thong under the mattress and hoping against hope that no-one had seen anything. Heart racing I sat and waited. The young warrior walked in bearing a bowl with a plate balanced on top in one hand. His other hand held a jug. The bulk of Ametsam's pet loomed threateningly behind him. He set the jug down on the floor and checked the bucket, which was still empty. He frowned at me but I hadn't needed to use it, so it was empty. He turned it upside down and set the bowl on his improvised table. The bowl and plate were wooden and the jug moulded leather with a waterproof inside lined with pitch. There was nothing for me to break and use either on myself or against anyone else. It had been the same every day I had been in the cell. The young man grunted and left without speaking a word to me but he did make a point of telling my guard that he would be back to collect my leftovers in short while. The door was yanked shut behind him and, as always, I heard the bolts being drawn. I hated that noise. It made me flinch each time I heard it. I hated the door being shut too. I investigated the food he had brought. The plate supported a chunk of bread, not fresh but full of seeds and grain. It smelled like it would be sweet too, which was a change. Under the plate the bowl held a thick soup which smelled richer and more sustaining than my meals had been recently. There was a wooden spoon shoved into it so far that the handle was almost completely under the surface. I fished it out and licked the spoon clean. My foot found the jug on the floor and it was warm too. It held a sweet fruit tea and it still had enough heat for it to be warming. I took a long drink of the tea and soaked the bread in the soup. I might as well eat it while it had some heat left and there was no way to test my thoughts before he came back. The soup wasn't that thick really but it had some vegetables and meat in. The bread was a little hard but soaking it in the soup solved that and it filled me. The tea in the jug was a warm sweet fruit flavour and I felt it warm me from the inside. I spooned up the soup and then used the last bit of bread to wipe the bowl clean. I saw no point in letting anyone know I was done, he'd be back soon enough. Sure enough a few minutes later the door swung open and in he walked, scowling. A freshly blooming bruise marred one cheek. It was still deep red and hadn't been there before. He gathered up the plate and bowl but left me the jug.

"For water," he grunted at me when I lifted it for him. I put it back on the floor and I thanked him. He smiled briefly. "Good luck," he mouthed and he turned and left. I sat heavily on the bed and listened to him walk away. I strained my ears to try and work out whether my monster guard was sleeping. I heard footsteps returning and my heart sank.

"Master Ametsam wants you." The voice rang out. "I am to stand in your place until you come back." There was some muttering after that and I guessed the warrior sent down here was less than impressed with his orders. The bulk of the thing filled the small barred window in the door and blocked out the light before it left. The human voice complained about the state of the space he was meant to be guarding and then went quiet.

When his face appeared at the window I shouldn't have been surprised. "Try now, you don't have much time," he hissed in at me. For a moment I was frozen in indecision. If this was a trap I would suffer more and probably die. I threw caution to the wind as his face dropped away. I stood on shaky legs. This was scary. This was a step into the unknown, a step in the dark with only trust to steady me.

I took the beaded leather from under the mattress and I went to the flowing water in the corner of the cell. I squatted down because it felt right and because the water was flowing thicker lower down and pooled on the floor there. I closed my eyes to try and find some calm, failed and opened them again. I held out the beaded leather and pushed it into the water. The glow that flared was soft like the sun seen from beneath water. The hand that came through the water gripped mine with warmth and friendship. She held my fingers round the leather and held it in the water as she pushed her head and shoulders through the water.

"I can't stay long," she whispered. "This is painful for me and I will be pulled back soon. I have a crystal to anchor your Portal in this realm. It must be used for you to go through and escape. I will leave it where you will see it in the place we both know." I listened and said nothing, fearing she would be gone in an instant. I nodded. The glade he had identified for us as the place I first stepped through to his realm. "I will find a way to get you out of this place and to where you need to be. Trust me?"

"Ah, that was quick." His voice raised outside the door. She thrust my hand from the water and the glow died. She was gone again but I had my hope back. The young man left muttering about getting given all the shitty jobs and the monster settled down to sleep. So did I with my beaded leather talisman pressed into my cheek.

*Kate turned over in her sleep. Jack's arm snaked out to snuggle her close and she half woke. She smiled sleepily and dozed off again. The bedroom door creaked open and Hayley poked her head in. "TV?" she mouthed silently and Kate nodded and Hayley slipped out, closing the door behind her.*

*Jack raised himself on one arm to stop the alarm clock before it went off and then slid from the bed to get dressed. Kate stirred at the movement and started to get up.*

*"No," he said. "You stay there. I'll get the kids up and to school. Get some more sleep." Kate didn't protest, she just shuffled further beneath the covers. Jack bent to kiss Kate gently on the forehead. She was already asleep again. A few moments later, Kate woke just long enough to panic that she was running late, hear the car on the gravel and relax back into sleep again.*

# 10. Escape

*Kate enjoyed a late breakfast alone. Blissful peace wrapped like balm on her soul.*

*Then over her second mug of tea she pulled out the manuscript, aiming to finish it before going to meet Lily for lunch in town. As she read the final few pages her cheeks flowed with tears. She felt the grief bubble and release like a bursting abscess.*

*Kate sobbed, a deep rising that left her wiped out and cleansed.*

*Finally, feeling calmer than she had for a long time, and finally believing that life might go back to normal, she wiped her face and put the card folder in her bag before heading for the car.*

I slept again. I don't remember dreaming. But I curled myself round that tiny kernel of hope that had just begun to grow deep in the most secret part of me. There passed a tense couple of days during which I was fed regularly by the young warrior who seemed to be helping me. The food was better than it had been before and I was suspicious enough to wonder if I was being lulled into a false hope. I didn't dare try to bring the beaded leather into the water again and the trickle seemed to be drying up anyway. I did drink from it as it was cleaner and fresher than the water brought in for me. I was dragged out of my cell several times and beaten physically or had the magical pain inflicted on me instead. From that there were no bruises but the needle-sharp hurts took time to die down after each session. I was in a state of constant ache and constant tense anticipation. Each time the door opened I felt the hope rise up. Would it be him, was it time? But each time it was pain or food. I felt like an animal, less than animal. I was dirty again and bruised. I just wanted it to all be over one way or another.

There were footsteps coming down the corridor and the door was opened by the monster guard who seemed to live there. The young warrior stepped through looking as sullen as he always did. I knew it for an act but I hated the thought of what would happen to him if we succeeded. He carried a bowl of broth and a hunk of bread.

His voice was barely audible. "Don't touch the broth. It's drugged and he always eats your leftovers." I nodded and took both bowl and bread from him. He left, stamping his way down the corridor as if this was the most distasteful task he had ever had to perform. He played his part well and I hoped he could escape punishment afterwards. I ate the bread slowly. It was hard and the broth smelled good. It was difficult to not eat it. The bread at least had the usual seeds in so was nourishing if not satisfying. It took the edge off my hunger. I sat on the bed and waited. I lay down and curled myself into a blanket. I figured I may as well rest while I had the chance. After a while the door opened again and the young man stepped in. I never knew his name, I had never asked.

"Griping belly, huh?" he asked as he took the full bowl. I curled tightly on the bed, trying to look sick as I caught his meaning. I nodded and grunted a reply without daring to look up and meet his eyes. He shrugged and left noisily. "You want to finish this then?" he asked as he pulled the door closed behind him. The confirming grunt was all I had ever heard from Ametsam's pet. I doubted it could speak. It had the intelligence to obey simple instructions but I wasn't sure how stupid it really was. It was certainly strong enough to rip a limb from my body if Ametsam told it to. So I lay curled as if sick and groaned now and then to enhance the effect. I don't know if it helped or not. I listened to it loudly eat the bowl of broth and then settle itself down to watch over me. The breathing I heard through the door got slower and deeper until I was sure it slept soundly. With a horrid slippery sound it slid down the wall and onto its side. I waited. I sat there ready and I waited. Those were the longest few moments of my life. I didn't hear him coming. His boots were soft leather made for stealthy work. I heard the bolts being drawn back and then the door opened slowly and quietly. I looked up carefully in case it wasn't him. He stood there in the doorway, eyes flicking back along the corridor nervously. He beckoned me and I didn't stop to think. I got up and went with him.

He led me away from the usual exit and I felt a panic rise inside me. But we rounded a corner and came into what looked like a dead end. He placed a finger to his lips in a plea for silence. I was happy to oblige even though I burned with questions. His hand walked along the stones in the wall until he found the exact one he needed. A slight pressure and a section of wall swung away. I almost laughed out loud then, it was so like being in a film. This was a special effect; I'd turn in my sleep and wake up in a moment. He pulled me close so he could whisper softly in my ear.

"This is yours," he whispered as he pressed something into my hand." I looked down. A fine silver chain lay curled in my palm. On it was a pendant. The delicate silver leaf was untarnished. I had all but forgotten it. Do you remember? The one you got me for my birthday just before this all began, just before I left you. I would have thanked him but emotion closed my throat. I saw from his face that he understood. "I can't come with you. I have to stay here and close this." His breath on my ear and neck was warm. "He'll kill me and my family if I am seen with you. You understand?" I nodded and clasped his hand in the way I had seen warriors do. He let go and gently pushed me out of the opening.

I stepped out into gloom. It was night but with that cold that said the night was coming to an end. The moon was almost fully dark and the clouds covered most stars. That worked to my advantage as I ran across the meadow, ducking low to try to avoid being seen. I reached the relative safety of the trees and paused to get my bearings. I had come out of the side of the fortress and I could no longer see where the opening was. It was hidden well. I carefully made my way through the trees until I was at the point where I knew my way. I moved slowly and as quietly as I could, going from tree to tree and trying to stay in the deepest shadows where possible.

I froze. A thought had sparked in the front of my mind and grew until it wiped out all else. I had left the beaded leather behind in my cell. The ice in my belly threatened to freeze me to the spot. I had hung all my hope on that small strip of leather. It contained the magic, the power I needed. My legs shook. I turned my head to look back the way I had come and I almost went back. There was no point running to the glade when the magic couldn't work. I had to try. I had to hope the Naiad could somehow make it work.

I carried on walking. I moved faster as I got further away from the fortress and deeper into the trees. Breathless I burst from the trees into the glade just as the sun was lightening the sky. Dawn. But I had stepped through at midnight, we had missed my moment.

The sickening plunge of my guts was becoming familiar as one thing after another seemed to go wrong.

The Naiad was waiting in the glade. "It's too late," I wheezed as I got my breath back. "Midnight is gone, and I forgot the talisman." She laughed at me, a gentle tinkling sound like the water that was her element.

"That was just to open a way for me to get to you in the stone," she explained. "You no longer need it." She took my hand and placed a small crystal in it, closing my fingers around it. "Plant this and a Portal will form. They are rare and the magic will attract him but you have a few moments." Her eyes went wide and she seemed to listen to something. "He comes. Go quickly and find your anchor. Set up your moment. Make sure your way is lit well. You will have to come back this time but we will hide you until the moon is fully dark and midnight comes again." I stepped away from her and laid the crystal on the ground. I pressed it into the soft earth.

The Portal flared in an instant. She pushed me towards it as I heard sounds of bulk forcing through the trees.

"Go!" she urged and I did.

I fell through the other side onto prickly green grass. I curled onto my side to pull myself a bit more together and I heard a door bang. Then came feet running down the garden. I hauled myself to my knees and an arm came round me.

Kate. You. The tears welled up then for both of us. I'd made it. But I knew it wasn't quite time to come back for good. I would need a few more hours to sort that out.

"I don't have long," I told you, looking round to see where Ametsam might open a Portal to come after me. "He's following me. He'll be here in a moment. Can you help me get back?" I asked, desperate. You nodded, speechless. "Meet me by the old oak, at midnight," I begged, picking the only place I know I could visualise properly and the spot where he had taken me all those years ago. I saw the Portal flare behind your shoulder and the pet's arm thrust through. I despaired. If he had me I would never get to this place again.

I was pulled away from you and I know you tried to hold on to me. It tore me apart to push you away but I needed you in your world to anchor my passage later. I was brutally hauled back through that Portal and thrown onto the grass in the glade. I retched dryly and let myself drop to the earth and I lay face down there as I waited for a fatal blow from either the pet or from Ametsam. I didn't even bother looking up or opening my eyes. My head spun with the rapid transit through two Portals in too-swift succession. The cool grass pressed against my cheek and a massive hand gripped the back of my tunic. I heard shouting and I was lifted high into the air. The world was spinning as I was held above the monstrous guard's head. I couldn't focus properly but it seemed to be alone. There was no flash of magic, no strike of power. I saw no blue. Ametsam had not come for me.

But the grey-green monster pet was formidable enough alone. There was no way I could wrench free of its grasp even at full fitness. I was far from fully fit. I had been not quite starved but fed only the minimum for survival. He had beaten me until I ached and the bruises were layered upon bruises and inflicted pain until I cowered at any raised hand. He had reduced me to nothing. If he had been there and beckoned me I would have gone to him. He controlled me so I had no free thoughts or desires of my own when he was there.

But he wasn't there.

The grey-green monster was being pelted with rocks thrown from the trees. I caught glimpses of green skin blurring between the slender trunks. There was certainly more than one person there but I had no idea who, how many, only that I was also being pelted as the pet turned and tried to dodge the hail of missiles. Flailing wildly I tried to make its dodging awkward, tried to throw it off balance. A rock hit me as it let go and I flew to bounce from a tree trunk and flop limply on the ground. I was stunned. My ears buzzed and my eyes refused to focus. The sharp pain in my ribs told me where the rock had hit and the other sharp pain in my back showed where I had hit the tree. Winded and gasping, I lay there as the fight raged around me. A hand grabbed my ankles and I think I screamed. I was dragged from the glade and I passed out.

I came to my senses lying in the dark. A cool hand bathed the sore spot on my ribs with a cold cloth. I heard a groan and realised it was me. I tried opening my eyes and it was still dark. A soft hand on my lips bade me be silent. My head ached and I was discovering more and more pains as I tried to move a little.

"Rest easy." The voice beside me was soft. I dragged my eyes open. A smiling green face greeted me.

"Naiad," I sighed. "Am I safe?" I asked. She nodded, still smiling down at me as I lay there. I tried to sit up but her hand pushed me back down easily.

"You have a day, less than a day of sun now," she told me. "We can open another Portal at midnight. From dusk on Samhain the time of our world and yours is locked together. When dawn breaks the link is lost. But at midnight tonight it will be midnight in both places at the same time and on the same day."

"How can we open another Portal?" I was confused, again. "The crystal was buried? It was lost." She silenced me with a finger on my mouth.

"It doesn't matter how," she said, and she was right. It didn't matter. "You have to rest and heal as best you may in the time you have." She slipped an arm under me and raised me up a little. "Here, drink this." A cup was pressed to my lips and I drank the liquid within. It was dark and thickly herbal but sweetened with honey. It hit the bottom of my stomach and dragged me down into the darkness again.

"She should be waking soon," I heard the Naiad's voice as I drifted back to the surface again. "The dose was light to help her sleep and begin to heal."

"I'm awake," I mumbled through thick dry lips. "I'm awake." My voice came clearer now as the fog cleared and I woke up fully. I sat up and found soft blankets falling away from me. I certainly hurt less than I had. The naiad was at my side in an instant. I swung my legs off the bed and sat there to allow my mind time to wake up and focus.

"You are feeling well?" she asked. I nodded. "Hungry? Thirsty?" She smiled at me, both of us perched on the edge of the bed. I nodded again, not trusting myself to speak. The room was gloomy but not dark. The bed was soft and reasonably comfortable. She left me sitting there for a short time while she went to fetch food and drink. When she came back the smells coming from the tray she carried were mouth watering. I could see something dark that could have been bread and it was steaming gently. There was a bowl of something wonderfully aromatic and a mug. She set these down just out of reach and brought a small pot of ointment to me. It smelled stringent and while not exactly unpleasant, definitely worth pulling a face at.

"It will help you begin to heal." She laughed at my suspicious face-pulling. "I like the smell. Sit still." I did and she smeared a thin layer of the thick, cold ointment onto my face, ribs and back. It was a shock and I felt the muscles tense painfully as the cold hit the skin. But as it sat on my skin it warmed slowly until there was a patch of soothing heat. I sat and let it relax me. She pulled my tunic back down and brought the tray over. "I'll leave you to eat," she said and left me alone. My bruises were definitely feeling easier and I ate the tasty bowlful with relish. It was salty and full of chunks of meat and vegetables. The dark lump wasn't bread it was a rich fruit cake. The mug contained more of the sweetened bitter concoction that I knew would make me sleep again. So I left it until last. Before risking drinking the sleeping draught I stood carefully on shaky legs and ventured towards where I could hear voices.

"We'll have to try and distract that thing as long as we can." A male voice.

"We will but it won't be easy." The Naiad's voice.

"It will be hard for us if he finds out who helped her." The male voice again.

"I know, but you know we must do this?" The Naiad again. "Wait, she's here." The Naiad came to the doorway where I stood. "You need something?" she asked me.

"I'd like some water to drink before I take that sleeping healing stuff you put in the mug." I smiled to take any sting from what I said to her. I know the tea was to help not harm but I would have appreciated some honesty.

"I will bring some," she told me, taking my arm and directing me firmly back to bed. I sat back there and drank the water when it came. Then I drank down the tea and slept again.

Some time later I woke feeling very heavy and aching in places I didn't want to think about. My life seemed so full of aching and pain that I simply sighed and turned onto my side. I squirmed slowly to try to relax the knotted muscles. I rubbed at my eyes to clear them of grit. I ran a hand through my hair and tried to ease some of the knots out. There was a glass of clear, fresh water on a small table next to the bed. I tasted it in case of more herbal concoctions. It was either simply fresh water or whatever was in it was odourless and tasteless. I drank it all. I felt the cold course down inside me and revive me in a way I never thought possible. It was very quiet. I wondered at that. I wondered if I should be suspicious of the lack of sound but I wasn't. I sat in the bed and just breathed for a while. I assumed I would be told when it was time and I may as well take advantage of the comfort I had.

My mind wandered a bit and I let it. I had kept my hope so firmly caged I hadn't allowed myself to think about actually getting back to you. Questions flooded through me. Would I really make it? Would Ametsam come after me? Would you welcome me back? How long had it really been? I suspected it was more than a few days from the look on your face while we were kneeling on your lawn. But how long had it been? Days? Weeks? Maybe months? How were the children coping? My head ached with the thought of facing it all and I could almost have convinced myself to stay.

The Naiad tapped gently on the door, just loud enough to attract my attention. "It is close to time now," she told me carefully. "The sun set a short time ago and the woods are in darkness. The moon is fully dark and the stars are hidden by cloud. It is a dark night, we should be safer."

"I don't wish you to be harmed, Naiad." I said. She smiled and shook her head at me. "I'm serious," I insisted. "If you are going to suffer then tell me what to do and I will do it alone. I will leave you out of this if I can."

"I cannot be left out of this now," she assured me. "He would defeat you and prevent you leaving if you tried to do this alone. I will be there with you and others will try to defend your Portal as long as they can." I nodded, reassured and grateful for her help. I swung myself out of the bed and stood. I wasn't shaking any more. The days sleep had rested me more than I knew.

"What happens now?" I asked.

"We eat," she said and took my arm to lead me to another room that looked like a kitchen. Kitchen is probably not the best word to describe that space. This was a room that was used for cooking, eating, storage and socialising. There was a table and some chairs alongside a bench seat carved from a huge tree trunk. The carpenter had followed the natural curves of the wood and simply smoothed them and then someone had added a scatter of hand-embroidered cushions. It was a beautiful room. She gave me a plate filled with bread, cheese and fruit. I ate hungrily. I knew I would need the sustenance before the night was out. I looked closely at what I could see of myself for the first time in days. My wrists were thin and bony. My skin was grimy and marked with injuries new and old. I was a mess.

While I ate the Naiad sat beside me. As I finished she spoke again. "It is still out there." I closed my eyes against the thought she conjured. The monster that was Ametsam's pet was still out there. We would have to avoid it. "We will do what we can to distract it, to turn it from you but I fear it has only one purpose in its lonely existence and that is to pursue you. Nevertheless we will try. We may be able to buy you some time." I shuddered at the price that time may well cost.

"Kate will be at the other end of the Portal." I told the Naiad every detail I could remember. "She has always grounded me, helped me to see clearly." I spoke of you and held your face close in my mind. I wrapped my arms round myself and recalled the feel of your arms round me before I was pulled back. "She will be there at midnight and I told her to light my way. It seemed to make sense. It's dark."

"It makes perfect sense," the Naiad reassured me. "She will be where the Portal opened when he brought you through the first time?" she asked to make sure she understood. I nodded. A tap on the door drew her gaze and she got up to speak to whoever was there. They were being very careful that I only saw the Naiad. I thought I understood why. If this failed I couldn't identify them to Ametsam. She came back. "It is time," she said simply and I felt a shiver run through me. I got up and followed her. She took me from her home beneath the stream, the home she kept for dry land people to visit and use. She took me to the darkest shadows she could find and cautioned me to silence. I tried but I have never been able to move that quietly. But I didn't speak. I know other shapes moved near us and I hoped they were the allies she had spoken of. They flanked us through the trees but I never saw them clearly. The Naiad pushed something egg-sized and sharp into my hand. Another crystal. I knew that I had to push this into the earth and it would trigger a Portal if I got it in the right spot. I clutched it tightly. I had no pockets and it felt safer with my fingers wrapped firmly around it. We went faster than a walk but not quite a run, more a slow jog. The shadows to either side kept pace with us.

There was a noise to one side and the Naiad shot out a hand to my arm. I froze. One of our shadows peeled off and ran, suddenly making more noise. The lumbering carelessness of the grey-green monster was easily heard in pursuit. I remembered to breathe again. She waited until the sounds of the chase had faded a little before pulling at me to move again. We reached the clearing with no further disturbance and I lay a hand on the rough bark of the old oak tree. The Portal flared.

I stood at the threshold and I hesitated. I could see the flicker of a candle flame and I could see you. I could just make out your silhouette. You were standing talking to someone or something but I couldn't hear your words. You shrugged. You checked your watch, a familiar movement. My heart lurched at it. You reached out a hand and pulled it back as if burned. You took a step back. Your head shook in disbelief.

I stepped back and turned to thank the Naiad but she was running back to the trees. The sounds of the monster came back louder and louder. The Naiad screamed at me to go, to go through now. The monster growled defiance and hate as it burst through the trees. It was followed by a hail of stones but they didn't even slow it down. It didn't turn aside or seem to notice them. It was coming and it wasn't going to stop.

"Shit," I swore. I ran for the open Portal yelling for you. "KATE! I'M COMING!" I felt the ground shake beneath my running feet as the thing surged from the trees and I saw over my shoulder that it ran for the Portal. It was right behind me. It was only a breath away now and I felt that stomach lurch of terror that I might not make it.

I fell out into your arms and it stumbled. The Portal was too small for it to pass through. It thrust an arm through and groped wildly. I had managed to open the Portal right in the middle of the trunk of the ancient oak. The power and solidity of age confined the Portal. Even so it would not be long before brute strength broke through. It reached for us both and then with a sizzle of magic it pulled back. I lay on the wet mouldering leaves, dazed for a moment. I was home.

*Lily sat across the table from Kate. They were in Nutters, their favourite café in town. Kate held out a plain card folder. Lily reached out and took the manuscript from Kate. "You're sure you're done with it?" she asked. "And you're sure you want me to read it?"*

*Kate nodded and let her fingers slide free of the card folder. "I finished it this morning. I wept buckets."*

*Lily smiled and slipped it into her bag. Kate grinned wickedly. "I could tell you how it ends if you like?" And the ripples of laughter filled the cafe. "Seriously, Lily." Kate wiped her eyes. "She was your daughter. You need to know what happened, what he did."*

*"Thank you," Lily said quietly. She got up and took their mugs over to the counter for a refill. While there she ordered some sandwiches for lunch, brought the mugs back to the table and sat back down.*

*"I finally feel like I can get on with my life," Kate said softly.*

# More Books by Sarah Barnard
# The Portal Series
# The Portal Between

Sam was gone, and no one knew where or why. Her car was found near the old oak tree, empty and abandoned. There was no sign of foul play, but also no sign of Sam, except for footprints that led to the oak tree...and stopped.

Two years later, her best friend Kate still cares for Sam's children, waiting for Sam to return for them. Then one day she does. "I don't have long," Sam says. "Can you help me?" Kate must help her return home from a place that is closer than you might think, but still a world away.

Sam's escape is just the beginning of her journey. Sam must go back to confront and defeat her abductor, leaving Kate to care for her children. Sam returns to the old oak tree, and the Portal to the world where she was held prisoner. In a whirlwind world of magic and monsters, where people and things are not who or what they appear to be, there are hard choices ahead, and Sam must learn if she's strong enough to make them.

# The Portal Sundered

Sam is now Mistress of the land beyond the Portals, abandoning her own children just as she had been abandoned as a child.

Haunted by her past and afraid of her future, she discovers that her nemesis had two sons.

One of them stands at her side, the other chooses to invade her dreams, refusing to allow her to forget. Every night she must relive the torments of her past until she can take no more.

With her magic out of control, Sam must decide whether to call on Lily for help, or if she can face this new threat alone. Either way, she must find a resolution before it's too late and Ametsam's son becomes the monster his Father was before him.

# Child of the Portal

Susan's mother commits suicide which releases her magic as she gives up her life, and threatens to destroy the realm she has governed. Her closest advisor, the Naiad, has also vanished and her healing influence is sorely missed.

Susan's own magic is developing as she approaches her teenage years and it confuses her as she begins to grow into the strong, young woman her mother would have been proud of. Even her newly discovered grandmother, Lily, is pleased with her, even though she refuses to teach Susan how to safely use the magic.

With the Naiad gone, nobody in control, and no-one prepared to fill either role, the magical realm is in flux and chaos threatens, and the situation only worsens when Lily is lost and assumed to be dead. It seems that all will collapse unless Susan can find Lily and bring her back to restore the magical balance. But is Lily still alive, and can Susan find the salvation that is needed for the conflict to end and for peace to be restored?

Lily must be found, only Susan can find her and only the Naiad can save her. Lily must choose where and who she wants to be to everyone who demands that she be someone else. Susan must decide who she wants to grow into, and who she wishes to claim as her family.

# The Heir

When Lilith's unborn child is threatened, there's only one place she can go. She flees her home to find her lost twin sister, the only person who might understand the choice that Lilith must make.

The Heir, the story of the birth of Lilith's first child is set three decades before the events of The Portal Between

# The Map and the Stone

Rhys is ten years old and he lives, with his mum, in a tiny house on a council estate.

Rhys is called a day-dreamer by his teacher at school, and he's always staying behind to finish his work.

But, out of the corner of his eye, Rhys can see something moving, in the trees, in the hedges, and then...

There's a Darkling on his bed, and it needs his help.

Haunted by the dying Darkling, Rhys must find the magical Nexus to find a way home for the last living Darklings.

# The Earthlink series
# EarthLink: Impact

What if they are up there, monitoring us, and the planet? What if the planet has grown, developed, become conscious in some way? What if just one person could hear that consciousness in pain? What if that one person had just crashed a stolen car after a night of drink and drugs?

Sage is eighteen years old and, ever since she can remember, there's been a voice in her head. She'll tell you that she doesn't hear voices, they don't tell her to do anything. It's just a single voice, and it doesn't speak, it screams. She hears an unending scream as if the voice is someone in constant agonising pain.

She's been told she's hallucinating. She's spent time in psychiatric care and on strong drugs that cut her off from her feelings, and she hates all of it.

But she's not hallucinating, the voice is all too real and Sage has been watched for years in the hope that she's not the only one who can hear. When Sage puts her life in danger, and it's clear that she is unique, intervention is necessary.

*News, updates, up coming book releases, and signed paperbacks can be found at Sarah's website: sarahbarnard.co.uk*

Printed in Great Britain
by Amazon